Erasure

Erasures

Contact Information:

Villa Magna Publishing, LLC
4705 Columbus Street
Suite 300
Virginia Beach, VA 23462

www.villamagnapublishing.com

ISBN: 978-1-940178-71-4 (pbk)
ISBN: 978-1-940178-72-1 (ebook)

Cover Design: Noel Hagman-Kiziltan

About the Author

Omar Imady is a unique blend of many identities: poet, historian, novelist, Syrian, American, exile, Sufi, 'Alan Wattsian', cat enthusiast, and impassioned coffee drinker. These diverse elements all come together in his ever-growing collection of eclectic fiction. Among his published works are The Gospel of Damascus, which was a finalist for the 2012 Book of the Year Award, and When Her Hand Moves, a compilation of three provocative and challenging novellas. He has also received recognition for his novels The Celeste Experiment and Catfishing Caitlyn, both winners of the 2023 Literary Titan Book Awards. His upcoming works delve deeper into the human experience of isolation and search for purpose in a world where answers are increasingly elusive..

Erasure

Omar Imady

PART I

I

Ray Blankenship was as predictable as his smartwatch and as gray as his tweeds. He was fifty-five, and acutely aware of the framework within which he would live to his predicted death at the age of eighty-four. Everything was factored in: from his genetic profile—his paternal predisposition toward high blood pressure and his maternal history of high levels of immunity—to his Wednesday morning ritual of inhaling vaporized nicotine over his first of three cups of freshly ground black coffee alternative, enhanced with CBD and vitamins B, K, and D, with which he washed down his assortment of brightly colored pills.

It was not just his lifespan that was subject to clockwork. New socks, a selection of pastel and primary shades, made of a sustainable bamboo cotton mix, arrived promptly at three-month intervals, a span calculated to factor in the durability rate based on his current weight, choice of shoes, laundry detergent, step count, and the fact that one in every twelve socks is lost annually. His dentist appointments were scheduled at intervals based on his diet, history of tooth decay, brushing habits, brand of toothpaste, and vape usage.

Once a month, a discrete package would be delivered to his front door at a time he was certain to be in so as to avoid it being left on the doorstep. This contained what might otherwise be called "disposable companions." Vacuum-packed, these arrived at intervals corresponding with the nightly activity levels recorded by his finger-chip, the choice of films selected on his streaming subscriptions, his hormone levels, and his seemingly chance encounters with Laura Spinelli, his middle-aged neighbor whose grocery deliveries were conveniently timed to coincide with when Ray left for and arrived home from work, and who, according to her purchase history, had a predilection for silk nightgowns that she was in the habit of wearing at all hours of the day.

Ray lived in an age that had mastered the art of predictability. He knew exactly what he had to eat and drink, and even how frequently he had to ejaculate to live another twenty-nine years. He also knew the price of each deviation; what it meant in very specific terms to increase his alcohol intake by even a glass, walk fewer than his daily seven thousand steps through the office corridors, or sleep in beyond nine on Saturday mornings. His decision to take up vaping five years ago, a choice predicted by algorithms to the very day of his purchase based on the hiring of his new boss, the sale on at VapesRUs, and his smoking habit between the ages of thirty-one and thirty-eight, eroded his lifespan by a total of one year, six months, and three weeks. He could, Ray was informed, offset this decrease by switching to organic vape juice, free of additives, delivered in a glass vape-stick for an additional price equal to three percent of his monthly paycheck. As it transpired, he decided against this; one year, six months, and three weeks was not worth an additional three percent per month to Ray. But this decision, too, had already been predicted.

Normality is determined largely by longitudinality. If something persists long enough it becomes the norm. Just as humanity had once come to accept electricity, the scientific method, air travel, and the internet as new normals, so too had they come to accept predictability as the norm.

There were those who railed against it, just as there were those who chose to live in Amish communities at the turn of the twenty-first century. But they were quieter now. They may still indeed have been shouting as loudly as they once had, but the volume of the ease that this new normal brought about was far louder than their insistence on a return to the 'age of freedom,' or whatever it was they called it.

Ray, like the majority of human civilization in 2049, had concluded that to live a life of predictability was to live a life that was free of sudden noise, free of sudden change; peaceful. The illusion of unpredictability still existed and, if one wanted, a state of cognitive dissonance could be maintained. The spur-of-the-moment decision to book a holiday was expertly marketed so as to appear in no way based on the bonus from work, the time of year, the price and availability of travel packages, and the weather forecast. The script was never obvious. That would ruin the audience's ability to suspend any remnant of disbelief. But it was never absent. No one ever went off-script. Their very deviances were already part of it.

And yet, Ray could not shake the sudden and recurring sensation of alienation that crept up on him in the netherworld between sleep and wakefulness. Much like one might crave variety in a sexual relationship—an inexpressible thirst for something new, a desire to shock, to be shocked, to try and be disappointed, to take a risk and be rewarded—Ray found himself mute in the face of his partner: life. He longed to dare to do the impossible. And yet, he did not know if daring were even possible anymore. A knowledge of a lack of happiness was not the same as unhappiness, he'd tell himself. And he'd sleep, wake, work, and wondered if, in the grand predictability of things, there was an algorithm that would tell him when this feeling would revisit him again.

The Principle of Predictability, otherwise known as the Principle for World Peace, was born first as a theory in the year 2039. It was proposed by Professor Gennifer Valcot, one of the first and only women to derive a universally applied principle. She published her article

"The Price of Predictability" whilst in hiding, in the final stretch of what had become seven years of world wars in which every side was losing in one way, shape, or form. Of the 195 countries that had constituted the global community, blood was shed in 187. Economies were destroyed, infrastructures torn to shreds, over six billion lives lost. The devastation was so acute that the extinction of humankind seemed almost imminent. War was fought at the physical, digital, and chemical levels. Science was once again harnessed for purposeful destruction. Viruses were manufactured to target specific genetic codes, malware was unleashed into the homes of enemy states, machinery went haywire—turning on its owners, planes fell from the sky, irrigation systems shut down devastating years' worth of crops, people quickly starved. The population of the Earth plummeted from nearly nine billion down to levels not seen since the mid-1900s.

Perhaps the hardest thing about war, for soldier and civilian alike, is not the killing, the hardship, the loss and sacrifice. It is the uncertainty. The fear. The not knowing when and from where one may, or may not, be attacked. A new arms race began. A frantic scramble for knowledge; knowledge of the enemies' next moves. Knowledge became the ultimate weapon. The only way to win was to know. To be ignorant was to be at risk, to descend into chaos, to live in fear. The world had lived in fear for almost a decade. Enough was enough. The solution was certainty, reasoned Professor Valcot, for the world to know in advance everyone else's next move. Not just governments, armies, and soldiers, but everyone. Humanity could not afford any more surprises. Any more chaos.

In the winter of 2040, devastated and exhausted, the leaders of all remaining regions met in a hotel conference room in one of the eight island states that had somehow clung to their neutrality and avoided the carnage unleashed by humankind against itself. Together, the leaders unanimously agreed to put an end to the factory that unleashed erratic human behavior. To put an end to the disorder.

It was easy to make such a proclamation. But unlike previous summits when similar words had been shared only to be reduced to empty slogans, this time, the surviving leaders of the world pledged their allegiance to the Principle of Predictability. In doing so, they agreed to permit the global use of a very specific series of algorithms with the capacity to monitor, measure, track, trace, and predict everything from politics and economics to medicine and sexuality. No domain of human activity was left without an algorithmic framework that defined its boundaries, trajectories, and risks. Nothing was left to chance because chance was dangerous. Chance became a chapter in history books. The present was predictable. And so, by extension, was the future. The fate of humanity would never again be risked, neither by the major nor the minutiae.

Along with chance, coincidence was also eradicated. Accidents, too, were minimized, and where incidents occurred, there was always an equation to explain them. Serendipity became a myth, and luck a heresy. Risk was as taboo as racism had once been. Magic and miracles gave way to kismet and karma of a uniquely secular persuasion. Everything was written, yes, by the very events that unfolded, which had in turn been predicted down to the molecule and millisecond, by their precursors.

In order to be monitored, measured, and micro-managed, human knowledge in all its forms had to be digitized, organized, and collated. Seven knowledge hubs had been created: Science, Literature, Policy, Finance and Commerce, Human Activity, Environment and Resources, and the Arts. Each of these spread their tendrils around the world with at least one branch in every remaining habitable zone.

Ray Blankenship was the managing archivist of the Literature Hub branch based in Zone 4, at the site of what had once been a large government library. Unlike other former cities around the world that became major targets during the years of conflict, the mass relocation of all officials and bureaucrats from Ray's city in Zone 4 at the beginning of the war had saved it from complete annihilation. Its buildings, other than those demolished by early missile strikes, were largely intact. Peace had brought back a trickle of civilians, as well as an expeditious influx of civil service employees, into the eerily empty government infrastructure.

The library complex, which had been vastly expanded in the euphoric adrenaline rush that had followed the armistice in order to fulfill the demands of the Literature Hub for ample space and digital capacity, was a ten-minute journey by electric travel pod from Ray's apartment. The original ten-story building that had stood on the corner of 15th and 94th—a warm, sepia, stone-colored block offset with cobalt window frames—had been replaced with a fifty-story colossus that stretched up to the kind of height that made it look from below as if it somehow arched right over the road itself. This towering tentacle was not alone in shadowing the streets. Following the pre-war population boom, the district had joined the national scramble to seize skyward real estate.

The population boom, as it so turned out, had been one of the major precipitators of the explosions that followed 2033. There had, of course, been speculation that the entire seven- year global cataclysm had been manufactured by world leaders as a solution to the demands on resources placed upon the earth by the

8.7 billion lives that depended upon it. But conspiracy theories were quickly clamped down upon in the new age of predictability and such theories, and those who spouted them, were soon silenced and forgotten.

Ray Blankenship lived on the twenty-first floor of 1499 94th Street in one of the three remaining occupied flats. Laura Spinelli lived in another. Bosworth, the elderly concierge, despite having the option to assume any one of the 152 vacant flats whose inhabitants had either been killed or who had fled to shelter with relatives in other parts of the world, lived in the small ground-floor apartment behind the reception desk. He spent most of his waking hours either polishing the buttons on his faded uniform or sitting at his desk scrolling a trembling finger up and down the page of his tablet—an almost paper-thin piece of technology that could be rolled or folded and popped into a small case or a pocket when not in use, but which would snap into a rigid rectangle when spread out flat.

The words Ray had exchanged with the elderly concierge would not have filled a single page of Bosworth's digital books. They communicated predominantly in nods. A nod up for greeting. A nod to the side for packages. A nod down for thanks. The only evidence Ray had of Bosworth's verbal abilities was from the cheerful conversations he overheard between the concierge and Laura Spinelli on her nightgowned excursions to collect her hemp milk deliveries. Ray would nod upwards to Bosworth, respond to Laura's chirpy greeting with something between a 'good morning' and a clearing of his throat, and make a beeline for the lift.

In the five and a half decades that Ray had lived, humankind had not once questioned their need for mirrors in elevators. On days when only Bosworth was at the desk, he would spend the fifteen-second ascent staring blankly at himself, wondering what the probability of his exact combination of looks—salt and pepper black hair, five-foot-eleven stature, and gray eyes—would have been when his mother and father decided one night, drunkenly or intentionally, to forgo their usual precautions and conceive him. On days when Laura Spinelli was in the entrance hall, he would stare at the floor.

Ray began and ended his daily commute with Rachmaninoff, played through small earbud inserts that sheltered him from the company of other commuters traveling in his assigned pod. At work, his office was clinically silent.

Ray was not a specialist in literature. He was a specialist in structure. It was his job to ensure that every piece of literature, text, work, manuscript, in any shape or form, was digitized, categorized, and archived.

Three walls of his office were painted an overly exuberant shade of buttercup. As part of the governmental effort to combat the lingering mood of despair and depression that had been the natural result of the devastation the world had witnessed, the Arts Hub had introduced The Color Initiative, promoting the use of pigmentation in all its forms to brighten and manage the moods of the population. Those who protested at the lack of science behind color psychology were soon accused of dampening the spirits of the populace and asked whether, since they were so anti-chromatic, they wanted to join the ranks of those in gray in the prisons, now confined to offshore ships.

Buttercup yellow had been selected from a vast array of shades to promote optimism, warmth, and the illusion that sunlight had somehow entered Ray Blankenship's subterranean office. The final wall was left white, not because white was supposed to promote balance and wholeness, but so that it could be filled with the interactive high-definition projection that appeared when Ray activated his desktop system.

With the press of a button, or rather a finger chip scanner set into a small indent in the corner of the white desk, the surface of which acted as a desktop screen, the wall was illuminated with a scaled display of the entire library. Each wing was color-coded according to category. At the center lay the original four buildings aboveground. A fifth building had been added to house the visitor's center, a Museum of Paper, and a number of administrative offices that had acted as depositories in the nationwide recall of all domestic books in the wake of the Great Burn, when the population, starving and desperate, fearing the Great Freeze of the impending winter of '39 had turned to using anything flammable as fuel.

The depositories were a strange place. Ray had always been fascinated as a child by the contents of people's bookshelves, but the contents of the boxes and bags handed over at reception were more intriguing still. They spoke to not only which books people had collected over lifetimes, but which books they could not bring themselves to set alight; those whose pages they could not bear to see curl and twist in the heat; darkening, blackening, then disintegrating in the flames, the ink often the final thing to disappear. Some households had not discriminated—Chaucer was burned along with chick lit. What was left was simply whatever had been on the highest shelf. Others had been systematic; started with pulp fiction, worked their way through their own self-imposed hierarchy of literature, saved only what they considered more sacred than heat.

On evenings when the Hub was quiet, and the prospect of returning home not yet appealing enough to warrant the energy it would take to leave his desk, Ray would search the archives for the books of his memories.

He tried to fill the imaginary shelves of his youth—his teenage years, the days spent reading in the shade of an oak, the nights spent under blankets with a finger-sized torch. He would search the digital files for Antoine de Saint-Exupéry, Kurt Vonnegut, Agatha Christie, Joan Didion, Colin Wilson, and Kenneth Graham, holding his breath before every click, before the number of copies left would appear on the screen.

Slipping the electronic pointer ring onto his chipped forefinger, Ray directed the arrow to the key at the side of the map and tapped Level 1. The buildings rose from the screen as though being uprooted from their foundations, and a new layer of halls, wings, and rooms sprung into view. This cuboid complex covered the entire screen, mile upon mile of excavated archival space and digitizing halls beneath the roads and streets of the city. Ray tapped the screen again. Layer 2 appeared. A further layer, smaller, of scattered rooms connected by corridors, housing Zone 4's share of the world's most precious archival entrustments. Though Ray did not click on Layer 3, he knew that beneath these lay the vast machines that fed both the monstrous ventilation systems and the digital hardware, the unseen side of the online; the wires and engines that fueled the seemingly ethereal world of digital platforms.

Ray tapped back to Level 1 with a flick of his finger and scanned the rooms.

A red light was flashing in East Wing 289. He tapped the wing and the screen zoomed in swiftly. The light was now flashing over a room in the eighth corridor. Ray tapped again and zoomed in. He read the room number that had appeared in glowing red letters over the map of the large copying hall that had filled the wall. The glowing light now hovered over a copying station in the far corner of the long, rectangular room. Ray switched to live feed mode and maneuvered the camera angle to hover over desk 112. The desktop, somewhat smaller than his own, was illuminated, as it should be, with a number of scanned digital pages showing on the surface. The book scanner, with its electronic page turner and instant Captur technology, was silent. Not unusual if a copyist was reviewing the pages and tagging the book before sending it to the archiving department. The trolley of books stood half full, waiting to be slotted into the tunnel portal that would deliver the books along a conveyor belt to the appropriate archival distribution desk.

The scene looked perfectly normal, everything in its place, just as Ray expected it, insisted on it, in his monthly briefings to his branch's employees. The only thing missing was the copyist.

Ray swiveled the camera around the room, scanning the backs of the other employees, looking for anyone out of place. He switched to the multiscreen camera view, checking the twelve monitors in the room simultaneously. Nothing out of the ordinary. Copyists from desks 23 and 24 seemed to be flirting near the water point in the wall, and desk 78 seemed to be playing a version of Tetris on his own personal tablet, which Ray could deal with later. But the copyist from desk 112 was nowhere to be seen.

II

In 1972, a team of researchers at MIT published a study predicting global societal collapse by the year 2040. They had been off by seven years. By 2033, with countries bursting at the seams with their swollen populaces, society had not collapsed but exploded. Whether it had been wisdom or cowardice that stopped those in power from unleashing their nuclear options, it didn't matter. They had found every other possible way to inflict mutually assured destruction.

By 2040, what was left of the world had a new set of predictions. There was a fifteen-year window in which to save the earth from complete environmental devastation. The earth, the overlooked victim of modern warfare—its surface pockmarked with building-sized craters, its soil and waters polluted with the chemicals that seeped into it from the canisters sprinkled over land and sea, and its protective ozone layer scorched and ruptured from the emissions of machines of destruction and the attempts to cope with the aftermath—was dying. And it threatened to take the survivors with it.

For decades before the war began, scientists had warned the world of its mortality. News broadcasts regularly featured updates on the impacts of industry and lifestyle on the climate with such a degree of frequency that the earth's inhabitants came to expect them as a feature of their daily life. Much like exposure to the effects of faraway famines and genocides produced compassion fatigue, the constant warnings became tiresome, and humanity, for the most part, stopped listening. 'Comfort over climate' had been the mantra. Until they realized that the warnings were no longer a threat; they had become the uncomfortable reality.

Floods of funds were injected into sustainable energy, the technology for which had been available but pitied as the unpopular younger brother of fossil fuels for decades. The world's consumption of meat plummeted, and felling trees became a crime against humanity. Not only were woods and forests awarded protected status, but the Growth Initiative was established by the Environment and Resources Hub that saw, within every bomb crater, hundreds of saplings planted. In the year before the war began, it was estimated that for every human there were 420 trees. By 2040, this number had been halved. Simulations predicted that without an increase of three hundred trees per human by 2055, the earth would suffocate.

There were several immediate consequences to the Growth Initiative. The most prominent was the disappearance of paper. All production of paper was immediately shut down. Within the space of a year, everything that had not already been digitized was transformed into an online version of itself. Proponents of the digitization movement spouted slogans of accessibility, consistency, and sustainability in their push to upload any form of the written word. It did not require any distinguished form of intelligence to realize that anything off-line fell out of the remit of monitoring, measuring, and micromanaging, and thus presented a threat. Paper was too unpredictable.

Were Ray to have had access to the stores of information on his personal and professional activities, he would have known that when Copyist 112 burst through his doors with a large book in his hands it would be the first time in two years, three months, and seven days that he had come into direct contact with paper.

"Mr. Blankenship…" the man blurted, adding after a fraction of a pause, "Sir…"

Half question, half apology. "I think you should see this…"

He yammered out a stream of words that he must have supposed constituted an explanation.

The blood pounding in Ray's ears deafened him momentarily to any sounds but his own startled pulse. He stooped slowly to pick up the pointer that had fallen from his finger in the shock from the slamming open of his office door, using the few seconds it took to stand fully upright to try to slow his racing heartbeat, sent into a frenzy by the loud bang of the door handle against the wall it had crashed into. He allowed himself a further few seconds to scan the sweat-speckled face of the man before him, whose eyes were now darting between the large yawning pages of the open book and the seemingly blank expression on Ray Blankenship's face.

"Who are you?"

Copyist 112 took a few steps forward and lay the book down carefully with his cotton-gloved hands on Ray's desktop, which had shut itself down into privacy mode when the door was thrown open. He stood back up, stretching his arms behind him in an attempt to assuage the cramp that had set in from carrying the heavy tome, and confirmed the conclusion that Ray had already reached concerning his identity.

"What are you doing here?"

The man took a deep breath. Ray assumed he could not have been older than thirty. Perhaps he was one of the lucky ones. Then again, perhaps he just looked young.

"I came in this morning to my desk as usual and picked up the next book to digitize. I placed it in the scanner, ran the machine, uploaded the files to my desktop, like I do every day. No issues there. But then…I checked through the digitized files, just like I do every day, and there was an error. Part of the page came up blank. *Weird*, I thought. So, I ran the scan again. Same result. So, I take the book over to the high-res individual page scanner over by Jill's desk and I put the pages down on the machine. Scan, send, check. Nothing."

Copyist 112 unclipped the tablet from the holder in his waistband and tapped the screen twice, swiped up, across, then tapped again.

"Here, see."

He proffered the tablet to Ray. Gingerly, Ray took the thin tablet between his fingers, glancing at the man's face, still flushed, and examined the screen.

Page 600 was there in full-color digital glory. Page 601 was all there too, as was 602. He looked up. The man's eyes were wide, expectant.

"Keep going."

Page 603 contained a full page of text. So did 604. But 605… The page began with text, small and seriffed, which flowed for about five lines. But then, at the end of a sentence, the words abruptly stopped. And in the middle of the page lay a blank space. It must have been about six lines long. Ray flipped back to the previous page to confirm its size. Six lines. Missing. And then the text resumed.

Ray opened a small drawer beneath his desk and pulled out a pair of white cotton gloves, mandated by the Hub in the event of any contact with paper so as to avoid the wear and tear of fingertips. He slid them deftly onto his hands, the fibers tickling his palms, and flipped the pages of the outspread book. The slightly yellowed paper of page 605 was filled with the ink-stained etchings of very obvious words. Ray flipped several pages ahead, and several back, just to be sure. Nothing seemed to be amiss.

"There must be a problem with your desktop software." Ray placed his chipped finger in the indent and his desktop glowed to life. He navigated his way through the flowcharts of folders that spread across his screen, each tap producing a new sprout of file options. "112…" he muttered.

He clicked the "Current Projects" folder and opened the most recent.

"That's the one," the copyist, now propped up against one of the yellow office walls, confirmed. Ray ran a finger between the fabric of his cravat and the skin of his neck.

The rushing that had pounded in his ears had subsided, but now Ray realized it had been replaced with a new, duller, heavier thud, somewhere just above his stomach. He scrolled down through the pages, stretched out on the wall before them.

602.

603.

604.

He paused.

605.

"How many times did you scan it?"

"Four."

"Same every time?"

"Same every time. I asked Jill to run it too. Same result."

Ray nodded and looked back to the wall screen at the blank space slicing across the page. He cleared his throat. "Thank you for bringing this to my attention. Leave it with me."

The copyist opened his mouth as if to protest his sudden exit and unresolved, unrewarded mystery, but Ray was already standing by the door, his eyes on the small dent in the wall where the doorknob had smashed into it with the copyist's arrival. As Copyist 112 sidled out sullenly, Ray closed the door behind him.

Alone again, Ray had the strange and uncontrollable urge to organize something. To straighten edges, align corners, pick out the drawing pins from the paperclip pot, tidy a stack of papers, alphabetize a filing cabinet, but in the post-paper age of screens there was little left in the way of office paraphernalia to provide such mindless therapeutic distractions. Ray sat in his custom-designed ergonomic chair and swiveled slowly, pivoting between a ninety-degree angle, his eyes fixed blankly on the empty space on the screen. He twirled the pointer on his finger.

A small musical note played from his desktop alerting him that he had five minutes before his system would shut down for the mandatory mental health coffee break that all employees were required to take twice during their working day. In a cheerful font, a panoply of options for hot beverages was presented on his screen. Somehow the oranges and greens made the thought of warmed milk alternatives and weak americano substitutes particularly unappealing.

Ray silenced the message, rose slowly to his feet. With a sideways glance at the dent in the wall, he pulled open his office door and headed down the long corridor to Room 369.

~

Monica Rush was sixty-three, though her smooth skin and dark, toned arms belied her age. Through the narrow window into her office, Ray could see her standing with her back to him, her tight ice-white curls cropped to a millimeter's length, and her leopard print pencil dress clashing violently with her scarlet stilettos. At first glance, Monica seemed to have embraced the Color Initiative far more than his own conciliatory attempts to match his cravat to his socks. But Ray knew all too well that this jovial vibrancy ran only so deep. Her choice of print was far more telling than her scarlet shoes and vivid hair.

He cleared his throat and knocked on the door. Monica turned around slowly. Seeing Ray through the glass, she beckoned him in with a flick of her pointer hand and sat down behind her enormous desktop. Her office walls were painted violet.

"Ray."

Despite the fact that Ray found himself more at ease in the brusque silences that surrounded his boss than the chatter that surrounded many of his colleagues, Ray felt the fabric of his cravat sticking slightly to his neck. His heart continued to thud in some misplaced section of his torso. Monica blinked slowly, waiting for him to answer what had been less of a greeting and more an instruction to speak. He noticed that the line of scarlet eyeliner above her top lid matched the shade of her shoes.

"I had an issue I wanted to run by you."

Monica tilted her head and narrowed her eyes, revealing the scarlet line again.

"It's probably just a technical error, but given its nature, and the fact it has yet to be resolved, I'm following protocol and am designating it as 'flagged.'"

Monica's expression did not change. Ray shifted on his feet and cleared his throat again.

"So, why are you here?"

"Here?"

"Yes, why are you here? If you flagged it, it will show in the system and will be dealt with. Why are you now standing in my office?"

"Well…it's not exactly a standard error."

"No?" Monica's brow furrowed slightly, but her almost imperceptible lean forward encouraged Ray to continue.

"If I might…"

He took two steps toward her desktop. Realizing what he was asking, Monica moved her chair back slightly and beckoned him toward the indent in the corner. Ray placed his finger in the groove and, recognizing his chip, the desktop sprang to life with his own settings. Page 605 appeared on the wall of Monica's office.

"You see, there seems to be a section missing in the scanned copies. The copyist ran them multiple times on both his system and a colleague's with the same result."

Monica's eyes were fixed on the page. She seemed to be reading the surrounding text.

"And the original?" she asked, eventually breaking the silence, looking now at Ray.

"The original is intact. There doesn't seem to be any problem with it."

Monica turned her eyes back to the screen. "I'll raise this with the Hub committee this afternoon. In the meantime, I suggest you look for alternative versions of the text and instalink this missing section to another edition. It shouldn't be difficult, given that it's the Old Testament. Even the Burn couldn't completely wipe out three billion copies."

Ray glanced quickly at the screen and then back at Monica, whose stare was now fixed on him. He ventured a question.

"Do you know what might be behind the error? I worried it might be something…sinister. The 2035 movement all over again."

Monica stood up from her large chair and switched the screen back to her own desktop. "It's far more likely to be a technical error. No need to be suspicious at this stage, Ray. Find the text in another version and create the instalink. And take your coffee break. The last thing I need are more branch mental health sweeps."

Ray nodded to her, then turned back and closed the door carefully behind him.

~

Ray had a vague memory of coffee once tasting slightly more bitter. The sharp edge, if it had ever existed, seemed to have been smoothed in the coffee alternatives that had replaced the crops wiped out by the impact of the overheated climate. It had an almost creamy texture, despite the fact that Ray always drank it black.

He kicked himself as he scanned through the digital pages of the book for not recognizing the obvious fact that this was a copy of the Tanakh, the Hebrew Bible, known to Christians as the Old Testament. He had never been anything other than nominally Christian before the war, but the language and numbering of the text should have given it away. He chalked up his obliviousness to the identity of the text to the fact that he had seen so many hundreds of thousands of pages in the eight years he had worked at the Literature branch that they all looked the same. Font may be bigger or smaller, margins wider or thinner, paper aged or new, but on a screen the words no longer jumped out at him as stories, merely as black symbols that fell under one sub-category or another, all needing to be scanned, located, and filed away into the monumental archives the Hub was creating.

It had not taken him long to identify which verses were missing.

1 Samuel 15:2-3.

He ran the verse numbers through the archives. Almost three thousand individual text hits were generated. He browsed swiftly through the tag summary at the side of the screen: seventy-six secondary texts and English translations, 1,895 exegetical works, and 954 polemical treatises of one form or another.

Ray scanned the titles. Like so many words alien to him for much of his life, he had become familiar with these terms in his time at the Hub. *Exegesis*, a fancy word for explanation; *polemics* meaning verbal arguments;

and *treatises*, which simply meant systematic writings on one subject or another. The words skimmed down the screen dizzyingly. He'd start at the top, he decided, as he opened the first text: *The Authorized King James Version*, first published in 1611.

He searched for 1 Samuel 15.

> *1Samuel also said unto Saul, The Lord sent me to anoint thee to be king over his people, over Israel: now therefore hearken thou unto the voice of the words of the Lord.*

Ray froze. He refreshed the screen. In a blink, the page was reloaded. Verse 1 appeared, as did every verse from 4 onwards. But verses 2 and 3 were missing.

Ray flagged the text, moved it to one side of his desktop, and opened another scanned file. *The New Revised Standard Version*, first published 1989.

> *1Samuel said to Saul, "The Lord sent me to anoint you king over his people Israel; now therefore listen to the words of the Lord.*

> *4So Saul summoned the people, and numbered them in Telaim, two hundred thousand foot soldiers, and ten thousand soldiers of Judah.*

Ray ran his fingers through his hair and unstuck the cravat from the back of his neck. He flagged the text and went back to the list.

> *New International Version*
> *Wycliffe Bible*
> *Young's Literal Translation*
> *The Voice*
> *World English Bible*
> *New Catholic Bible*
> *The Message*

Lexham English Bible
Living Bible
International Children's Bible

Ray opened them all. All seventy-six existing digitized versions of the Old Testament that had survived post-2035. 1 Samuel 15:2-3 was missing from every single one of them.

Ray's hands were shaking slightly as he moved to the folder of exegetical texts, struggling to remember the exact series of events that had led to the 2035 wave of cultural terrorism that had been unleashed around the world. The thinking, as far as he could remember, and as far as there was real thought behind any terrorist movement, had been that a victory over the enemy was only complete if not only their present was destroyed, but also their history; not only their civilization, but their heritage. It was important not just to wipe out rival regions by crippling them physically, but by depleting them intellectually. From what he could remember, libraries had become primary targets. Sprinkler systems were hacked and activated, heating systems exploded from mechanical power surges, ventilation systems pumped with mold spores. Billions of books were destroyed.

Then the hackers turned their attention online. Publishers' archives were infiltrated and wiped; viruses ravaged digital reading platforms. The counter-terrorist attack had been swift and robust, but not fast enough. Digital stores took a huge hit, with an estimated fifty-eight percent of online texts disappearing or irretrievably corrupted. Ray daren't search for the origins of the 2035 attacks. He knew anything related to those events would be "hot" and would appear next to his profile to be discussed at his next evaluation. He returned to his search list and opened the first exegetical text.

His smartwatch beeped with a blood pressure warning, and a notification appeared on his desktop screen advising him to take a series of deep breaths. Ray swiped the popup away and returned to his search. By the time the lights in his office started to dim in replication of what might have been a deep crimson sunset glow had his office not been some twenty-five feet underground, Ray had scoured forty-eight exegetical texts, commentaries, and polemics for the missing verses. In not one file did he find them. He flagged them all, manually overrode the automatic light dimmers, sat back in his chair, and cracked the knuckles of his left hand.

Outside his office, through the small window in the door, he could see a trickle of people filing through the corridors toward the main entrance where their transport pods would be waiting. Soon he would receive a notification that his pod had arrived. He switched his desktop mode to Do Not Disturb.

In the absence of a scanned copy or digitized version of a published book to instalink the missing verses to, the next best option would be to provide a link to a verified website. The surge of "fake news" in the late 2020s had presented a dilemma to ruling powers of liberal democracies: Did the right to free speech entail the right to lie? They did not know the answer. A compromise was reached. Rather than ban or delete content deemed to purvey false or inaccurate information, governments instead invested heavily in verification software. Anything posted, published, or promoted was run through a series of verification checks to authenticate the information by cross-checking it with existing facts and data. Everything written and disseminated on the internet was awarded a verification status: verified; unverifiable; false. Of course, there were inevitable flaws and loopholes in the system, and with the devastation wrought upon digital archives in 2035 the system was fragile. But, if Ray could find something verified pre-2035 and instalink the scanned document to it, this was at least a temporary solution.

He ran the verses in the search engine. Almost four million hits. Ray let out the breath he had been holding and clicked on the first link. A Bible search tool. He scrolled down to the verses.

"Fuck."

~

Monica was not in her office. Ray knocked on the door of the adjoining room. Her secretary, who seemed to be juggling a phone call, emails, and a flashing desktop message, waved him in with a harried look on his face, but could tell him nothing other than the fact that his boss had left for the committee meeting three hours ago and hadn't returned.

Ray's tablet vibrated, at the same time that yet another message notification flashed on the secretary's desktop. They each read their messages quickly. The secretary finished first and looked up at Ray through his bright-yellow rimmed spectacles, which Ray knew in an age of laser eye surgery were simply for show.

"Looks like you got your answer."

With a downward nod of thanks in his direction, Ray headed back out into the corridor and hurried to the elevators.

The office of the Literature Hub's Zone 4 branch director general was located on the first floor of the original library building. Ray ran his fingers through his hair and fiddled with his cravat. The large wooden door was opened before he could knock. Monica was sitting in the far corner in a high-backed armchair in front of one of the huge arched windows. It was dark outside. Ray could see the street lamps' blurred glow through the thick anti-UV coating on the panes. The room was startlingly juxtaposed against the bright varicolored interiors of the underground offices. It was faintly lit by the desk lamps that reflected off the polished mahogany surfaces of the paneled walls, the large round conference table, and the wide desk behind which sat a man whom Ray presumed was the director general.

It took Ray a moment to identify precisely what had seemed so odd about the room, in addition to its ornately decorated ceilings, somber color scheme, and dim lighting. In the corner stood a large bookshelf, lined with leatherbound volumes, their titles embossed in gold lettering that caught the dim light. Ray wondered if they were real, or whether this was merely a sophisticated version of the fake windows so many houses now installed, lit with dimmer bulbs to give the illusion of sunlight without the risk of ultraviolet exposure.

Monica looked up from her tablet as Ray stepped cautiously into the room. He wondered whether he should take a seat but saw nowhere convenient to sit. The director seemed to be deep in conversation with whoever was speaking to him through the earpiece. Monica turned her head to watch him. The director nodded, giving low, nasalized hums of approval every few seconds, and finally finished his call, tapping his earpiece to end the connection. He turned to Ray.

"This is him?"

Monica nodded. "Ray Blankenship."

"You're the one who raised the first flag?"

He now seemed to be addressing Ray, who answered. "Yes, sir…" The strangeness of the director's question suddenly struck him. "I raised the flag this morning… but…"

The director had now turned back to Monica. "Has he been sweeped?"

"He has, sir. He's clean."

Ray flushed at the news that his entire online record had been reviewed in the space of the last few hours. Everything from his subscriptions to his purchase history, his fingerchip log, productivity stats, and medical records. It took high-level clearance to obtain access to an employee's private data, and while the results of any searches had to be kept confidential—except where a breach of law was concerned—the effect was still enough to raise the hairs on the back of Ray's neck, to which his cravat had started to stick again.

"Good. Debrief him. Set him up as branch liaison. They'll need someone to help them navigate the archives. Mr. Blankenship, we need this solved quickly and quietly. Under the counter-terrorism regulations Article 25, you are required to give the Hub your full support in ensuring any threat is either disproven or eliminated."

Ray looked from the director's piercing stare back to Monica, who rose to her feet, her heels making indents in the thick pile of the checkered gray carpet.

"If I may?"

The director nodded and Monica pressed her finger into the groove of his desk, filling the wall opposite with an AuthaGraph map of the world. Unlike many other things to which Ray had become habitualized since the Declaration of World Peace in 2040, the AuthaGraph still took him a minute to adjust to. Perhaps it was because, like most people, he looked at world maps in his day-to-day life far less than he actually realized. Perhaps it was because it gave him the strange sensation that East had suddenly become West and West had become East, and that everything he had known before the war was only a reflection of the truth. The AuthaGraph map, designed by a Japanese architect, Hajime Narukawa, in 1999 had been largely ignored, even when it won the Good Design Award in 2016. But in 2040, hailed as the most accurate two-dimensional map ever to be designed, it was globally adopted in place of the Mercator map, which the world had used since the sixteenth century.

Perhaps the most radical difference between the AuthaGraph and the Mercator maps, other than the obvious rotation and placement of continents, was the size of many landmasses, in particular Antarctica. Whereas on the Mercator this stretched the entire length of the bottom of the map, giving the impression of a gargantuan expanse of ice, the AuthaGraph shrank it down to its true proportions, a continent roughly the same size as Australia, and rapidly shrinking. This was the official line behind the adoption of the AuthaGraph.

Much had been made in the campaign of the necessity of preventing any further shrinkage of this store of greenhouse gasses—everything from slogans encouraging the installation of solar panels, before they became mandatory, to cutting down on the consumption of unnecessary products. Digital billboards blinking across zones blared high-definition slogans: "The Price of Ice Is the Ice!" Chastisements in the form of advertisements for Frink, an eco-friendly ice alternative. "There's not as much as you think, so put Frink in your drink!" Ray had often suspected, though had never dared suggest, that ice had very little to do with it. Of course, environmental concerns had been top of the World Congress agenda, but it did not take a conspiracy-inclined mind to wonder if the real aim was to present the true proportions of certain countries in order to shrink the egos of would-be super-powers.

"Your flag was logged at 10:15."

Monica was aiming her pointer at the red dot that was hovering over their location. She moved her finger. Ray followed her pointer. "At 10:37, a flag was also logged at the Zone 2 branch." A red dot now appeared over the next nearest habitable landmass.

"Same segment, same text." Monica now tapped on a tab at the side of the screen.

"By 12:08, thirty-two flags had been raised."

A swathe of dots, which seemed to be multiplying rapidly, spread across the seven zones in the middle of the map. There was at least one dot in every remaining inhabitable region of the planet. Those areas shaded in gray—claimed by the rising sea levels, bombed into oblivion in missile attacks, or sucked dry into deserts—remained eerily empty.

"Same segment. Now different texts."

"That's what I was coming to tell you."

Monica turned from the map to look at Ray.

"I searched every possible primary source of this text, and it's disappeared from all of them. I ran the search through secondary sources too, everything we have in the digital archives, and they all returned blanks."

Monica and the director exchanged swift glances.

"So, I ran a net search for verified pages." Ray paused.

"And?" The edges of the director's nostrils seemed to have turned white.

"Nothing. Just blank space. The text has gone."

Monica had now opened a live tab with a list of flags under the tag "1 Samuel 15." "You logged all the texts?" She scrolled down to Ray's flag listings.

"Yes, although I stopped at the web searches. There were just too many. But I checked dozens."

Monica looked back at the screen and watched as the dots continued to multiply across the strangely distorted map. "This is serious. The committee has initiated the establishment of a probe team to address this. It's been raised to a Code Ochre. We need to contain whatever this is and repair the damage. I believe you still have the original print text in your office—is that right?"

Ray nodded.

"I need you to bring it to my office immediately. The probe team's designated lead investigator is on his way from Freedom Point. He will be here by 6:00. I'll need you here then, too."

"You are to cooperate with him fully, Mr. Blankenship. We have reason to suspect that the malware originated here in Zone 4 since this is where the reports were first raised. And I need a list of anyone in your department you might suspect of being involved in this in any way." The director was now standing. He was shorter than Ray had expected.

"Copyist 112 has already been taken in for questioning," Monica added. Ray could not tell whether the tightness at the corners of her mouth conveyed a steely determination, or the faintest hint of unease. He restrained the sudden urge to look at her calves.

Ray knew as he left the office to collect the book still lying on his desktop that his every move was being monitored. He had nothing to hide, but the knowledge of his surveillance was uncomfortable, akin to the sensation, in the age of transparent windows, of seeing a neighbor's curtain twitch. It made his every action suddenly seem somehow not his own, as if he were playing at being himself. He shook his head, ran a finger around the edge of his cravat, now faintly damp, and keyed in his code in the elevator.

The corridor lights glowed into life one by one as he made his way toward his office. It was not the first time he had worked late, being the last to leave the department, but tonight the underground level seemed echoingly devoid of any life. Perhaps it was the specter of an enemy, a word all but omitted from common parlance, or perhaps it was the vast depths of solid earth that were compacted against the walls that gave the corridor its grave-like feeling. Whatever it was, Ray was relieved to reach the bend in the corridor that led to his office.

He rounded the corner and froze. There on the floor just by his door was a dark shape. He felt his heart thumping in his throat. The figure, having sensed his presence, now rose to its feet.

"Mr. Blankenship," called out a female voice. Ray let out a shaky breath. "Jill?"

"Yes. I'm so sorry, did I startle you?"

She was heading toward him now. Copyist 228, with whom Ray was only on a first-name basis because she had been assigned to give him the copy room induction when he had first joined the department. He had not seen her since she had tried to make small talk with him in the main foyer not long after, but she was unmistakable. Ray could make out her features across the corridor now that she had pulled down the hood of her maroon sweater, which clashed violently with her cyan hair and orange lipstick. Ray was not sure she had entirely understood the point of the Color Initiative, which only added to his irritation at having been spooked.

"Not at all. I'm afraid I'm very busy, Jill…"

She was standing in front of him now, just a few meters from his office door. Ray looked behind him, unsure who or what he was checking for.

"Mr. Blankenship, you need to see this."

Jill had pulled out her tablet and was swiping across the screen with a dimpled finger, the nail of which was painted fuchsia. "I flagged the issue, but I was worried it got lost. And after what Barney showed me this morning…I thought you should see it." She looked up from the screen at him. "Copyist 112," she added, answering the question Ray had hesitated to ask.

"You found missing text." Ray tried to mask his frustration with the fact that Jill was still blocking his way through the corridor with a thin smile.

"Yes, that's right." She nodded eagerly, still fiddling with the tablet. "I know I had the tab open… One second…"

"We've already identified all the other scans with the segment missing, Jill. I appreciate you bringing this to my attention, but your flag will have already been noted and filed under the Samuel 15 tag. I must just…" He turned to try and edge his way around her large frame.

"Oh, but it's not Samuel 15." She looked up at him and held out the tablet.

"I beg your pardon?" Ray stared at her.

"It's not Samuel 15, sir. Look."

III

Ray could feel the soft heat of the shape next to him and felt the gentle movement of the thin cotton sheet tug against his skin with every low, simulated breath. The itch in his eyes, the tension in his shoulders, and the ache in the heels of his feet were dulled now, his brain flooded with the sweet headiness of endorphins.

And yet, he could not sleep. It may have been the awareness that he had only four hours before he was required to be back in the department that contributed to his insomnia. Perhaps it was the slight streak of discomfort that the disposable companion, which had been delivered to his door twenty minutes after his arrival, had skin of a deep umber and short, cropped curls. Or perhaps it was his awareness of the words still inked on his palms.

The page Jill had shown him only a few hours before was from the *Coverdale Bible*, published in 1535. He recalled the scene, the page as crisp in his mind's eye now as it had been before him in the corridor.

He had scrolled down the page Jill had shown him, wishing somehow that this was all a bad dream and that he would wake up and the dreamscape software would identify the underlying threads from his everyday life that had precipitated this mental performance and reassure him that the world was still just as predictable as it had been the day before. It might tell him that it was natural for a man of his age to start worrying about forgetting things, which was all that the missing segments represented, but that protein treatments now existed to waylay the onset of cognitive decline. Or, perhaps, the software would tell him he was looking on some deep subconscious level, for an excuse to arrange a meeting with Monica, for some way to be a hero. But the slight heat from the tablet Jill had handed him and the glare of the screen in the dim corridor had dispelled any suggestion that this was simply a cerebral scenario he had conjured in his sleep. Ray had taken note of the chapter at the top of the page: Luke 19.

> *26But I saye vnto you: Whosoeuer hath, vnto him shal be geue: but from him that hath not, shal be taken awaye euen that he hath.*

> *28And whan he had thus sayde, he wete on forwarde, and toke his journey vp to Jerusalem.*

Verse 27 was missing. The faint mottling of the scanned pages glared through the surrounding verses like a scar across the page. Ray had cleared his throat.

"You have the book? The hard copy?"

"I left it in my office." Jill's eyes had seemed to gleam with either fear or excitement, Ray could not determine which. "It was too heavy to carry."

Ray's brows had furrowed. He would have preferred to have been able to take both texts back to Monica. "I need to see the text," he had told her, shifting again to see whether he could maneuver past her politely.

Lying now in the uncomfortable warmth of his own body and blankets, Ray slid his left hand out from beneath the hips of the figure next to him. He peered at it in the darkness, the irritation he had felt coming back to him, slowly edging out what was left of his post-coital serenity.

"You'll think I'm incredibly clever." Jill had beamed in response to Ray's disappointment that she had not brought the book. "I tried writing down the words on my desktop, but every time I saved the file it came back corrupted. I tried to write it and turn it into a Captur image but the same thing happened. Of course, the sensible thing to do would have been to write it on paper, but who has paper nowadays?" She had laughed. Ray did not mirror her joviality. "So, I dug out an old pen I had lying in the bottom of my rucksack. I have them as keepsakes, you know. They sell really well on the global marketplace." Ray had cleared his throat and looked down the corridor toward his office door again.

"I thought to myself, *Where oh where could I write this?* And then it hit me. As a child, I remembered my mother would always write her shopping lists in a place she wouldn't forget them."

Jill held up her hand to Ray's eye level. There, scrawled across her palm in blue ink, was verse 27.

As for those myne enemies, which wolde not that I shulde raigne ouer them, bringe them hither, and slaye them before me.

Ray stared at her palm, thinking quickly. "Jill, do you still have your pen?"

In the darkness of his bedroom, lit only by the blue light of his tablet charging in its port in the wall, Ray peered again at the shaky words he had written across his palm. He was not sure how many years it had been since he'd seen his own handwriting. It looked almost foreign, like another language. Standing in the corridor, silent but for Jill's heavy breathing and the sound of his own thunderous pulse, he had copied the words carefully from Jill's hand to his, trusting that the eagle eyes required of a copyist meant that she had not made any mistakes.

He slid his right hand next out from under the sheet and held them up next to each other in the dark like some strange ritual of prayer. Jill's handwriting was etched across his right palm. Her fingertips had felt warm when she'd held his hand steady and pressed the nib to his skin. Standing in his office, with 1 Samuel 15 before them, it had been her turn to write.

2This is what the Lord Almighty says: "I will punish the Amalekites for what they did to Israel when they waylaid them as they came up from Egypt.

3Now go, attack the Amalekites and totally destroy all that belongs to them. Do not spare them; put to death men and women, children and infants, cattle and sheep, camels and donkeys."

Monica had been in her office when Ray had knocked.

Ray felt the heat of the pillow beneath the back of his neck as Monica's features swam before him in the blue-tinted darkness.

She had beckoned him in from her seat behind her desk. He was carrying the book under one arm and a tablet in the other.

"There's been a development."

Monica looked up at him, her dark brown eyes fixing him in her gaze.

"Copyist 228 found me just now and brought it to my attention." He had shown her the missing verses on his tablet. Something, Ray was not quite sure what, passed over her face. An invisible hand that either left something there, just under her skin, or had taken something away.

"Luke. New Testament." She paused, as if trying to recollect something. "Do you have the hard copy?"

"I don't. The copyist left it at her station."

Monica frowned and closed her eyes for a fraction longer than a blink. Ray noticed that the scarlet lines above her lids were duller than this morning.

"But I do have *a* copy."

She looked up at him, one eyebrow raised into a steep arch. He held out his palm.

From a locked desk drawer into which Monica keyed a code, she withdrew a sheet of plain white paper. She'd held his palm flat against the desk with her fingertips, the nails pressing into his flesh slightly as she copied the words in solid print. Ray had ignored the thin quiver that ran down from his ribs to below his navel.

"Smart work, Ray."

He realized he had stopped himself from ascribing true credit for the idea, and wondered now, with a flush of shame, whether he should have.

"See you back here in a few hours." Monica had walked out from behind her desk to the far corner of the room. Ray watched her as he stepped out backwards through the door and noticed she had taken off her shoes.

In his bed, Ray lingered on the scene, recalling the soft sound Monica's feet had made as she trod across the carpet. He rolled over onto his side and slid a hand around the warm frame next to him.

Freedom Point had been built on the highest spot of habitable ground at the farthest point from any ocean or body of water. The large anti-UV dome that had been built over it, harnessing the latest transparency technology, was supported by huge columns that, in their ingenuity, the architects had turned into high-rise office towers so as to give the illusion of normality. The climate stabilizers within what could easily have become a living sauna were fueled by tidal power, the solar farms that had spread across old grasslands, and the forest of wind turbines installed across the shores of deserted regions, which converted the hazardously blistering winds into usable energy. It was the first global capital city in the documented history of humankind. All governmental power had been centralized into the hands of a presidential committee elected biannually by representatives of the surviving global community. Regional powers had proven too dangerous to be trusted. So, the devolved zone governments that now sat in what had once been the seats of power were little more than placeholders.

Ray had never visited Freedom Point. It was not a place where one just turned up. Permits usually had to be applied for years in advance, and vacancies for positions in the vast networks of bureaucracy that sat in their lofty repurposed-steel towers, when they did become available, were snapped up instantly. Competition was fierce when there were more than a thousand applicants to choose from.

Marshall Fielding had somehow defeated such competition to rise through the echelons of bureaucrats to become a high-ranking anti-terrorist investigator at the Department for Prognostication, or Prognostics as it was fondly known by its inhabitants, the largest department in the capital. He donned the mantle of his new position as lead investigator with an air of ceremonious pride.

In the Literature Hub of Zone 4, Fielding seemed to fill the entirety of Monica's office, leaving little room for Ray to edge in through the door. He was in the middle of reeling off a long list of capital directives in Monica's direction. Ray was not sure Fielding had even noticed him enter the room until he finally turned. Fielding was aggressively good-looking. His strong, square jaw, wide smile, heavy brows, and crisp blue eyes were almost unsettling to look at. Ray stared at his forehead so as to give the illusion of eye contact and counted three faint lines across it. He could not have been much younger than Ray. He wore a magenta handkerchief in his suit pocket, which matched his patterned tie. Ray couldn't help wondering if his briefs were the same shade.

"Ray, this is Lead Inspector Mr. Marshall Fielding. Mr. Fielding, this is Ray Blankenship, our head archivist."

Ray noticed she had not introduced him with a formal title and tried not to wonder whether the ocean blue boots and necklace she wore today matched any of her hidden garments.

"Oh, just Marshall, please." Fielding flashed Monica an almost iridescent white smile as he put out his hand to shake Ray's. Ray knew better than to be fooled by such charm. The man's grip was tight and ice cold. "You know, my ex-wife was called Ray." The smile stayed fixed as he scanned Ray's face, pumping his arm up and down, before finally releasing his hold.

Ray nodded, unsure as to why, under any circumstances, this information would be relevant. He felt the urge to wipe his hand over the front of his tweed suit.

"You're the one who first flagged the missing text?" Fielding asked, though it was more of a statement than a question. "And you logged a second flag that same night." Fielding was helping himself to coffee from Monica's refreshment booth. Ray glanced at Monica but failed to detect any response from her expression.

"I did. It was brought to my attention by a copyist."

"She's being held for questioning at the moment," Monica added. Ray scratched the palm of his hand with his fingers. "The other copyist is still being held."

Fielding looked in Ray's direction.

"Ray's been swept," Monica added.

"Yes, yes, I had a look at the results on my way over. Interesting…" Fielding dunked a biscuit into his coffee.

Saliva rose sharply in the back of Ray's throat at the thought of Fielding reading through his sweep results. He kept his gaze steady on Fielding's forehead but was sure he felt Monica glance in his direction for a fraction of a second. The shadow of a silicone silhouette flitted briefly before him.

"Nothing suspicious, obviously, or you wouldn't be here." Fielding looked up at Ray and flashed his teeth again. A chunk of wet biscuit fell into his cup.

"We've set up Room 359 as the investigation hub. Ray has been assigned to assist you, Mr. Fielding. I will be available whenever my services are needed, but in order to maintain the necessary discretion I will attend to my usual role unless otherwise required." Ray noted her refusal to address the inspector by his first name.

"Smart thinking," nodded Fielding. "We need to ensure that staff are unaware of the investigation. Let the copyists' colleagues know when they arrive that they are off sick, or have gone on training or something."

"A plan is already in place." Monica, Ray realized, had made her way subtly to the door. He stood up and straightened his jacket. Fielding rose too, tipping back the remnants of his coffee and biscuit sludge, and strode to the door as if leaving had been entirely his idea. They followed Monica down the long, winding corridor to Room 359, whose walls were painted a shamrock green. Having seen to it that Fielding had access to the desktop system, and that they had everything they required, she pulled the door closed behind her. Ray could hear her footsteps receding down the corridor.

"Formidable woman." Fielding raised his eyebrows at Ray. "Formidable boss," Ray responded.

Fielding's wide smile stretched across his face. "Of course. Now, Ray, let's get to work, shall we? We need to weed out these goddamn terrorists."

"You're sure it's terrorism?" Ray furrowed his brow. It was true that when Jill had shown him the second missing segment his mind had jumped immediately to that conclusion, but he had expected the inspector to have a broader array of potential leads to investigate.

"Assume the worst. It's the only surefire way not to be caught with your cock out." Fielding didn't laugh. "If we've learned anything from seven years of war it's that people are not just capable of anything, but willing to do anything if they believe in it enough. And the world can't risk people's willingness. Or their beliefs. There's too much at stake. That's why the punishments for terrorism are the harshest they've been in decades." He kept his gaze fixed on Ray, his jaw set, as if analyzing the impact of this allusion to the underworld of law and order had on someone he still had not determined was completely innocent. Ray felt inexplicably hot. Fielding's face broke back into his wide, toothy beam.

"Here's what I need from you, Ray," he said, sitting down heavily into the desk chair. He counted off the instructions on his hand as he reeled off his list. "And some coffee would be great. I'm two cups down."

The wave of loathing that had been building in Ray crested, turning his cheeks a shade of scarlet that the Color Initiative may have associated with tenaciousness, but which Ray experienced as a surge of heated though silent indignance.

"Sweetener?"

Fielding looked up from his desktop as though surprised to still see Ray standing there. "Uh…yeah, sweetener. Two." He held up two fingers in a wide *V*. Ray nodded, swallowing the sharp saliva that persisted in welling up in his mouth, and turned toward the door.

"And a dash of creamer, too, would be great," Fielding called after him.

~

The woman at the hardcopy archive desk had long copper hair that hung down over one side of her face. She wore an emerald green turtleneck sweater and large gold earrings in the shape of seashells. Twenty years ago, Ray might have been captivated by the fiery hue that had once constituted only two percent of the population's genetics, but the proportion of redheads had increased dramatically over the course of the last two decades. The higher pain thresholds of redheaded women, coupled with the ability of redheads of both sexes to produce higher levels of vitamin D in short spaces of time, had caused a spike in their survival rates. This apparent evolutionary advantage had become so celebrated during the postwar era that men and women who had not been put off procreation by the devastating era of destruction flocked to salons in swathes to dye their locks a shade of red in the bestial hope of attracting a mate.

The archivist's freckles seemed to confirm her authentic redheaded genetics, although Ray was faintly aware that cosmetic surgery now offered a facial treatment that promised permanent freckled features. Ray wondered if she might be one of the small sliver of society who had not been irreversibly scarred by the global genetic genocides of children, afflicted by diseases that targeted those with the weakest immune systems, wiping out newborns and the very young, and decimating the population of those over seventy who had not fallen victim to the bombs, toxins, and cyber-attacks that wreaked havoc in homes around the world. Those few men left of childbearing age who had not been conscripted, wounded, or killed on the battlefield, it had emerged in the years after the peace treaty was signed, had for the most part suffered irreparable damage to their sperm counts as a result of the biological effects of many of the weapons.

Only twice in his life had the thought of having children occurred to Ray in any profound manner. The first was not long after the birth of his godson, at what would once have been called a christening, but which had become known in more recent decades as a "naming ceremony." It was not so much the child that had caught Ray's attention, but rather the look that passed between Sarah, the child's mother, and Charles, the father, Ray's closest college friend. Whatever it was that passed between the two of them, Ray had never seen the likes of before, certainly not between his parents, and though he often looked for it, never again had he seen it pass between Sarah and Charles.

The second was on his forty-sixth birthday, which coincided with the week the treaty was signed. In the moment peace was declared, the distraction, and the excuse of the war, had been lifted, and Ray had found himself in the fifth decade of his life almost entirely alone. Granted he was not unique in his isolation, but it occurred to him in that moment that despite having survived an event that had wiped out almost the entire population, were he to die now, there would be no one to remember him.

The archivist uploaded the digital map to Ray's tablet, handed him a pair of gloves, a facemask to protect the pages from any extra humidity or foreign microbes he might exhale, and drew out the most expedient route for him to collect the hardcopies of the texts that Fielding had requested from the cataloged titles. Ray was used to seeing the archives in digital format, color-coded according to category. He had forgotten how dark they were in real life. Kept away from light in meticulously controlled temperatures, the dry air kept clean of dust and micro-particles so as to preserve their paper, the books sat behind miles and miles of plexiglass screens. They lined the shelves like bricks in a multi-colored maze illuminated only faintly by the dim lights that glowed briefly over Ray, detecting his motion as he made his way along the course of the map, pushing the square plastic cart before him.

He paused in front of the first shelf marker. The lights glowed brighter, sensing he had stopped. He pressed his fingertip to the lock. A faint green beam somewhere inside scanned the chip identifying him, and the glass pane clicked gently open. Ray reached inside, scanned the code on his tablet, and grasped the book's spine. It slid out with a whisper.

J. B. Phillips' *The New Testament in Modern English*, published in 1996. He placed the book on the cart, closed the glass screen, and walked on, his footsteps clicking on the dark floors. It occurred to Ray that a mechanized system for book retrieval would have been infinitely more expedient, and he wondered if he should propose this at the next departmental development meeting. At the same time, books were so rarely retrieved once they had been archived that the financial resources that would be required to install such a system might be hard to justify, particularly in light of what might be a serious cyber breach. In any case, Ray was, in that moment, grateful to be away from Fielding and in among silent pages.

He pulled the next book from the shelf. *The New Testament 1534,* translated by William Tyndale. He resisted the urge to pull out other titles, scan their contents, and wonder about the long-dead authors of so many of these books, books that had lined the walls of his father's office, books that had always been piled high at the side of his mother's bed. As he had grown older, his childhood interest in reading adventure stories and sci-fi tales had dwindled and he had instead taken to collecting cookbooks, one of the few types of books that he had always felt was still worth owning in print, and which had been the last he had contemplated burning for fuel. It was with great sorrow that he had parted with his collection when the Print Drive was announced. His prized copies of *Mastering the Art of French Cooking*, *Larousse Gastronomique*, *Nose to Tail Eating*, *The Moro Cookbook*, and *The Art of Eating Well* he had handed over with the pain of leaving a lover. He was miles from the gastronomy section, but the temptation to reach out and run his hands along the spines like he had done when selecting a book from his long kitchen shelf was all too tempting. He reached out his fingers to the row of titles before him, daring himself to touch them.

A muffled thud broke the silence. Ray jumped, maneuvering swiftly to catch the book that almost fell from under his arm. He held his breath. There was silence. The blood was pounding in his ears. Perhaps a book had fallen inside a shelf somewhere, though Ray was sure the cases would be soundproof. He strained his ears.

A stifled mumbling seemed to be coming from beneath the shelves. Suddenly, Ray's feet were illuminated in a pool of light.

"Shit!" came a sharp breathy exhalation.

Ray's heart was pounding. The archivist had not mentioned that anyone else was down here. Perhaps they had come in after him. Slowly, he crouched to his knees and leaned his head down to floor level.

Beneath the shelves, in the handspan gap beneath them that allowed them to be wheeled further or closer apart, lit by the faint glow of a tablet torch, Ray saw a hand groping. He scanned the length of the floor beneath the shelf and spotted the dark shadow of the book the hand must have been searching for. It had slid almost all the way over to his side of the shelf. Ray reached for the book and withdrew it slowly. He read the title: Marmaduke Pickthall's 'The Meaning of the Glorious Quran.'

A sheen of cold sweat had formed on Ray's brow. Perhaps it was just an archivist filing away a hardcopy once their scans were complete, he thought. There was no reason for him to worry. Certainly nothing for him to fear. He crept around the edge of the long row of shelves, careful not to step into the motion sensor area of the first light of the row. A few meters away, illuminated in the yellow glow of the overhead, Ray could make out the shape of a large behind, the belt of the turquoise trousers slipping down, the material taut over the bent form of the man reaching desperately under the shelves.

"Can I help you?"

The man, startled, bumped his head on the underside of the shelves, grunted, and dropped the tablet he was using to shine a light into the darkness. He shuffled unsteadily backwards on his hands and knees. He stumbled to his feet and pulled up his straying belt.

"I was just… I needed to…um…"

Ray walked forward slowly. "You dropped this." He half-held the book out to the man, who made to reach for it, a look of relief passing across what Ray could see of his masked face. Ray held the book steady, inches from his fingers. "Who are you?"

The man looked from the book to Ray. "Gerry Stains. Umm…Copyist 43. I've been working on the Eastern manuscripts section. I was transferred from…"

"And what are you doing down in the archives?" The mixture of fear and adrenaline gave Ray a sharpness in his questions that surprised him.

"Well…I…it's hard to explain." The man ran a hand over his sweaty forehead. Ray's expression remained steady, though the throbbing pulse in his ears had not subsided.

"I was scanning the text, the one…" He nodded in the direction of the book Ray was holding. "…this morning, and everything was going fine until I came across…" He fumbled for his tablet, and remembering he had dropped it on the floor, he bent to retrieve it. He tapped the screen and pulled up a page. "…this."

He held out the tablet to Ray. There, among the small, printed lines across the page, lay a sliver of blank space. Ray swallowed.

"I thought perhaps if I found another copy I could instalink the blank section, or just replace the entire thing…. I don't know, I panicked. Please don't fire me. I really need this job."

"You noticed this this morning?" Ray was scrolling through the pages with a shaking finger.

"Yes. About an hour ago. I ran it multiple times, and I…" The man's voice caught in his throat.

"And there's nothing else missing?"

The man shook his head.

Ray swallowed again. He handed his tablet to the man, who took it with a quivering hand.

"Am I fired?"

Ray did not hear his question. He opened the book he was still holding and flicked through the pages.

There it was. Another missing verse, typed out in ink, absent from the screen.

Then, when the sacred months have passed, slay the idolaters wherever ye find them, and take them (captive), and besiege them, and prepare for them each ambush. But if they repent and establish worship and pay the poor-due, then leave their way free. Lo! God is Forgiving, Merciful.

Ray tried to swallow again, but found his throat was dry. He looked up at the copyist, who was now wringing his hands before him.

"You'd better come with me."

V

At the turn of the year 2030, the newly formed World Muslim Congress celebrated the fact that Islam had overtaken Christianity in having the highest proportion of religious adherents. Street parties were organized across the Middle East, broadcasts were beamed across the world, a monument was unveiled in Islamabad, and the pope shook hands with the Congress secretary general. They hailed the strengths of their interreligious dialog, their outreach programs, and the staunch efforts of their religious leaders in maintaining the creeds and practices of their congregations in the face of the rising tide of atheism, and more importantly, apathy toward religious systems.

Twenty-seven percent of the world's believers ascribed to Islam in comparison to Christianity's twenty-three. What these figures ignored, and what the celebrations entirely and unconvincingly overlooked, was the fact that this twenty-seven percent represented a proportion of what had become a severely emaciated segment of the global population, and that what had really contributed to the shift in proportions was nothing more than higher birth rates in Muslim-majority countries. For every child that was born into a Christian family, 2.7 were born into a Muslim one.

The forecast for religions had been bleak. While the previous decade had seen eighty-five of every hundred people in the world claiming at least nominal adherence to one faith or another, by the end of 2030, this had shriveled to a mere fifty. It was not for want of initial recruitment and appeasement efforts by religious figures, nor the blurring and bending of their rules and red lines in an attempt to coax back followers. Religion had become a relic, a useless antique no longer passed down through families. It was taught in Western schools now not as religious education, given its perception as divisive, but rather as a module in history courses. Its irrelevance to a generation nurtured in the image of online influencers and viral miracle workers was exacerbated in the wake of increasing global hardships, which had been co-opted into the pre-existing narratives of enmity and hate espoused in areas of the world where religion, nothing more than a mask for the Machiavellians who wielded power, still ruled.

The space religion claimed was eroded rapidly by liberal democracy and its associated freedoms; congregations were replaced by online communities, prayer by affirmations, purpose by potential, miracles by explanations, the divine right to rule by free and fair elections. Religion posed more problems than it solved. It played a marching tune in an era in which no one traveled by foot. By the time the church decided priests could cohabit, they found their pews were empty. By the time mosques opened their main prayer halls to women, they found no women wanted to come.

The tides of religious defections swelled across the globe. There were many chips at the flint of religious establishments that sparked incendiary flames, but none quite so fierce as the story of the Arab prince's daughter. From the barricaded fortress she had made of an airport restroom in Milan, with the hammering blows of security guards against the door demanding she cooperate with the authorities in her return to her home state, she sent out a viral message encapsulating her plight. It was not a plea for help, but a war cry. Waving the black headscarf she had removed as a banner of conviction that she would not surrender, she vowed she would not return to a land where she would be killed for abandoning her family's beliefs, a land where her abusers and rapist not only walked free, but whose hands were shaken for their attempts to bring their wayward daughter back in line. Her screams spoke for the millions of women who had been silenced as she had, who had been told to keep their legs crossed and their mouths closed unless their husbands demanded otherwise.

The response, decades delayed, finally arrived. The United Nations adopted her plight, and the woman whose face was once covered became the poster child for emancipation. Her book, *The Freedom to Be Myself*, captured the essence of the pursuit of her contemporaries—the search for an uninhibited identity. The cover, a rare picture of her in her traditional black attire juxtaposed against a snapshot of her on a beach wearing nothing but a bathing suit—or as the tabloids dubbed it, "From Burka to Bikini"—was seen as an open affront to her countrymen, who issued edicts calling for her death by various barbaric means, and a promise to her countrywomen: escape is possible.

Women across Muslim states, who could no longer bear the fact that they were being denied what the rest of the world was seemingly taking for granted, swapped their hijabs for hashtags and joined the movement of religious refugees, beseeching the powers of liberal democracy for safe passage from hell to the promised land of freedom. Hotlines and international corridors were opened, guarded by UN regulations on freedom of religion, which in this case meant the freedom to have none.

The exodus of Muslim women, celebrated across what had been Europe and the United States as a liberation movement, was steadily being matched by a current of Christians who could no longer escape the imagery that was so ingrained in everything from religious festivals to architecture. Already burdened by its associations with historical oppression for which the Church had dragged its feet to apologize, it could not atone for its most significant sin—the insistence on the masculine mask of God. God was a He, and He had a son, and no amount of linguistic manipulation or ecclesiastical gymnastics could convince congregations otherwise.

Other religions suffered similar fates, hoisted by their own petards in their attempts to preserve matter over meaning, substance over spirit. Judaism had long been reduced to an ethno-specific sect. Conversions into the faith were rare and were mostly discouraged. Though philosophically, Buddhism had been seen as more compatible with modern values, its peaceful reputation as a faith that until that decade had escaped the associations of the Abrahamic religions, was irreparably undermined by the genocides perpetrated by followers against their non-Buddhist neighbors. Hinduism was met with a similar wave of abandonment following the massacres of Muslims at the hands of its adherents across the Indian subcontinent.

Those who left seeking spiritual asylum on the shores of the West were welcomed into a society that was rapidly shedding itself of the trappings of ancient traditions. Pockets of the faithful remained, but they were swiftly shrinking. Under threat from this growing tide of non-belief that spanned the spectrum from anti-theism to indifference, religions turned inwards. In the same way that those subjected to waves of invasions often incubated their cultures behind closed doors, religion tightened its belt and stiffened its resolve. The outside world, with its science, materialism, liberal values, and individualism, was the enemy, and the dwindling communities closed ranks and celebrated their superficial successes.

War delivered the final blow. Whereas previous world conflicts had seen civilians flock to their churches and temples in search of salvation, the bombs and bloodshed of 2033 and the years that followed sounded the death knell for religion. Where possible, and by those who cared, blame was laid at the feet of faith, at its millennia-old insistence on division, on a simplified reward-punishment perspective regarding global events, and on its repression of women, which had led to the very birth rates that caused the shift in religious demographics. Those who didn't care simply forgot. Religion was relegated to the realm of lullabies and fairy tales, half-remembered, stumbled upon with confusion every once in a while, like an old and faded shopping list in a bag at the back of a closet.

By 2040, the celebrations were silent. The geography of those areas of the world where religion had still prevailed were hit hardest both by the fighting and by the extreme climate conditions exacerbated by the conflict. Those who joined the mass migrations left their faith behind them with all the other baggage they could not carry. The older generations, those who remembered religion as a fully formed thing, were hit hard by the chemical and biological attacks that targeted weakened immune systems. They took their faith, where it still lingered, with them to the grave. Those who clung to their dogma did so surreptitiously, afraid of the stigma it carried, afraid of retaliation attacks in the new era of equality, which meant, in so many words, homogenization. Demoted to the ranks of myths and magic, of the archaic and obsolete, religion was no longer worn on one's sleeve, around one's neck, or on one's head.

It was important to note, as the Global Summit was careful to do, that religion was not outlawed. It was not censored, nor was it banned. People were free to read their religious texts, practice their rituals, and journey on their pilgrimages. All they asked, or rather insisted, was that such practices did not impinge upon the rights of any other individuals or communities. What they did not say was that there was no need to impose a ban of any kind. Apathy and apostasy had done the work for them. Nietzsche had been right. God was dead. And religion had killed him.

And yet, the questions persisted. The prince's daughter may have found freedom, but she did not find answers. No one denied the fact that her choice to embark on a career of mainstream soft pornography was an expression of her newfound independence. What she had found was what secularism had promised: the complete and uninhibited right to construct, create, and curate her individual identity. It offered materialism, in the fully fledged sense of the word. It never offered meaning. It did not claim to. And those who fled never found it. Just as they had never found it in the now empty mosques, the vacant pews, the silent synagogues. What had been missing from the cages of dogma from which they escaped had not been found in the wilderness of the West, a land that had turned against its own answers. The questions persisted. In the quiet before the war, they could be ignored. But the booming of the bombs, the pain of the viral pandemics, the relentless stream of agonizing images amplified them. The questions became louder. Secularism was silent. It had never promised answers. God was dead but his absence was more powerful than his ancient presence ever had been.

"It was only after we buried you," the poet Joan Fernandez wrote in the wake of the war, "that we realized you were not in the tomb."

Much as Mayan temples had been visited as tourist sites before they had been destroyed by a wayward missile, any churches, mosques, and temples in the Free World became sightseeing spots and museums or were repurposed as housing, hospitals, or schools, recognizable only by the architectural features—domes, minarets, and steeples— reconstruction could not smudge out.

The only unadulterated remnants of religion were its books. Books, the surviving tomes of which had now been gathered across the world to be stored in the vaults and archives of the Literature Hub branches. Millions of copies. Books now in the process of being cataloged, categorized, and digitized, so that every word read by anyone anywhere could be monitored, documented, and fed into the algorithms as data points upon which personal and global predictions could be based. Books, from the Bible to the Book of Shadows, from the Tipitaka to the Tanakh and the Talmud, from the Quran to the Vedas and the Upanishads, from the Guru Granth Sahib to the Avestas, from the Tao Te Ching to the Book of Mormon, sat in silent rows in the underground archives of each of the seven habitable zones. Books that had governed and guided for thousands of years. Books that had described and depicted, fashioned and fortified a framework for the cosmos. Books that held a history of now obsolete icons, vexing images, and archaic language. Books from which words were now slowly disappearing.

VI

Ray pressed his finger to the almost imperceptible indentation on the tempered glass wall of his bedroom. A small green light blinked beneath it and a split appeared in the mottled, marbled design. Slowly, the panel slid forward. A light came on behind it, and Ray drew the panel back to reveal the contents of the hidden closet.

Seven faces stared out at him, their expressions suspended as though caught in a photograph. The air trapped in the long, thin space smelled faintly of the perfume his high school teacher had worn, which had taken him three months to track down.

Disposable companions, as their name suggested, were meant to be discarded after a week of use. Ray, however, had determined that this was, in theory, the equivalent of a maximum of seven "intimacy sessions," as the packaging had called them, and sent them for recycling only when this number had been fulfilled. He returned them to the closet each time sanitized and fully clothed, which gave him, for a brief moment, the feeling that he was meeting them only in passing.

He ran his eyes across the figures' rigid postures. The woman, who looked remarkably like a young Jane Peters, a sophomore he had shared a seminar row with, and whose silicone replica had arrived on his doorstep after he had spent a Saturday morning looking her up on social media. Next to her was a dark-haired model in a bank clerk's uniform whose arrival was met by Ray with a mixture of uncomfortable arousal and a conviction to avoid the bank for the next six weeks. Ray stood her up straight, smoothing out the jacket of the companion next to her, a young man who it had taken him a total of four months to activate before he slid in between the sheets next to the warm figure and had turned off all the lights.

He glanced quickly over his latest companion, for fear that activating her might blur the new memories he had formed only that week of Monica: her insistence on addressing Fielding by his title, and her use of his own full name. A glazed look fell over him as he sank deeper into the memories, the image of the sharp, curved lines around her calf muscles, and the tiny white curls at the nape of her neck that stood out starkly against her skin.

The model in the clerk's uniform sliding back toward the shoulder of the young man drew Ray from his rapture. He reached for the final figure in the row. She had been his first, and Ray was loath to part with her. He drew her out only when he knew a deep part of him needed quieting, when only the safety he had once found in childhood would do.

He stood the figure at the foot of his bed and pressed his finger to her wrist. Her shape softened, as though Ray himself had breathed life back into her. He felt the warmth rush beneath the silicone skin, the color rise to her cheeks. Though it was possible to program companions to have a voice, Ray had always chosen silence, worried that words would break the illusion that everything else was designed to create. The heat, the moisture, the texture, the scents. Her face, the one he had imagined so many times alone in his room after school, formed a smile. The heavy chest rose and fell gently beneath the cotton shirt. He undid the first button. The scent of the perfume flooded his nostrils. He folded the shirt neatly and placed it on the armchair in the corner of the room. Feeling around her waist he undid the clasp and zip of her skirt, revealing her silk petticoat. The cotton skirt whispered as it slid over the fabric across her thighs. She raised her foot to step out of the garment. Ray folded this too and lay it carefully on top of the shirt. He pulled back the bed covers and guided the figure, now clad only in silk, gently down onto the bed.

The thick, reinforced windowpanes kept out any noise from the street outside, and silence seemed to pad the walls of the room. The only sounds were the figure's simulated breathing and Ray's own stream of breath. He slid his hand along her legs and up toward the heat radiating from between them.

It was the furrowing of Fielding's brow and the fact that he hadn't blinked once when he had brought the new text to Ray that had told him that Fielding considered him, on some level, a suspect. It was clear to him now.

The sensation of the figure's feet wrapping around him, clasping together at the base of his spine, mingled with Ray's stream of consciousness. It pulled him deeper, the smooth skin ever so slightly sweaty now against the pressure of his chest. The floral notes of the perfume were merged with a citrusy tinge.

His mind raced through all the possible reasons he could imagine a person might want to erase verses from the texts of three dying religions. There were easier ways to make a statement in the era of globalized communication, he thought. And the variables involved in coordinating the discovery of these three texts in the same place made the likelihood of success extremely low. Someone would need to know precisely which texts were being digitized in which locations, which could only mean it was someone from within. Or at the very least, someone with a source on the inside. But by now network checks would easily have uncovered whose desktop system had been used.

They would be fools to think it was him. It would be far too obvious. If he were behind these text deletions, then it would not make sense for him to expose himself.

Unless they thought he was pulling their bluff, diverting attention from himself by making it appear as though he had merely discovered them, and in the process lifting the lid on whatever message was supposedly being conveyed.

Ray felt a wave of nausea flood his stomach and threaten to push up behind his ribs. He swallowed, resting on his forearms, and became aware that he had softened inside the hot, slippery silicone. He rolled over onto his back and felt around in the sheets for the fleshy wrist. From somewhere inside the hidden mechanisms of the figure next to him, whose knees were still parted, came two faint beeps. She rolled over, propping her head on her palm, and smiled at him. The silicone folds of her stomach fell in soft, comforting curves. He felt her hand maneuver between his legs, and he closed his eyes, feeling the fabric of the pillow cool the sweat at the back of his neck.

He strained his memory back to his school days, groping for a trace of the histories of religions. If his tattered recollections served him correctly, the verses seemed to have disappeared chronologically. Judaism being the oldest of the religions, then Christianity, followed by Islam. He struggled to remember whether there had been a religion newer than Islam. If there had, he reasoned, and this was a pattern, surely this would disappear next. He had not heard anything from the department since he had left at the end of the week, though if he were under any sort of suspicion it was unlikely he would hear anything at all. Though perhaps there were no developments precisely because it was the end of the week, and whoever was behind this could only work from inside the archive walls.

The grasp of the fingers around him tightened slightly, and their motion quickened. He was unsure whether he felt the smooth metal of the wedding band or if his knowledge that it was there informed the intensifying sensations. Monica didn't wear a wedding band. He had checked with a discreet flicker of his gaze during his first meeting with her. That being said, bands were uncommon even among married couples, and had been for some years. Marriage as a concept had given way to civil partnerships, a declaration of intent to commit, and a financial arrangement in the absence of longevity fulfilled. But Mrs. K, as they had known her, he, and the boys in his eighth-grade English class, had been married to the geography teacher, to whom Ray had taken an irrational dislike upon the discovery of this fact. He had wondered, with a deep and seething resentment, whether Mr. K's picture sat smiling in the locket that nestled in the fissure that revealed itself when she lowered her head to check his composition.

Ray exhaled, feeling his body tighten, as though a turning key had been twisted somewhere in his neck and every sinew in his being had been tautened. He pressed his knees together as her motion quickened still, and he dug his nails into the skin of his palms.

Ray had always been confused by the fear of death. If it were true, and the inescapable end did feel anything like the flood of indescribable sensations—somewhere between sunshine on skin and an electric shock—surging through him, then death could only be a welcomed thing. A moment of ecstasy.

The fear of dying, on the other hand, he could understand. He had seen more than his fair share of dying. Pain, disease, prolonged suffering. Agony. This he would do anything to forgo.

His breath came in short bursts. Had he been asked to describe the sounds he made in those moments, he could never have obliged. It was impossible to exist within himself in that instant. He was never sure quite where he went, but for a fleeting second he knew he had departed, and nothing existed but release.

It was with reluctance that Ray began to return to himself. The figure lying beside him had rested her head on the pillow now. He slid his leg between her thighs and pulled her close to him. He could never bring himself to kiss any of the companions that had been delivered to his door. And returning to his body, it was not the intimacy of a lover that Ray sought; it was shelter for a moment longer from the arrival at himself. The inevitability of it all and the certainty of it all. He buried his face in the figure's chest and inhaled her scent.

The serenity did not last. It never did. The endorphins ebbed; his thoughts returned. Coming back to himself was always crushing. It carried with it the dreadful weight that he spent his waking hours desperately trying to avoid. The scenes of horror, the crippling violence humans inflicted on one another, the emptiness, the pointlessness, the hollow eyes of those who survived, filled only with distraction, the sour taste of discontent that never left him, the clawing at the cavern inside of himself that he knew each and every person he met could feel but would never admit to sharing. Because to admit was treason, a betrayal of life. He rolled onto his back and pushed the figure away from him.

~

"I need to see you in the director's office, Ray."

Monica's hair was now an electric blue, and the lines along her eyelids were silver, matching the shifting tones of her wide- legged pants, the knife-edged crease slicing down from her hips to the lapis lazuli toes of her barely visible shoes. There were holes at the shoulders of her shirt, which was covered in a willow pattern.

A cold trickle dribbled its way down Ray's spine. He put down his coffee cup and followed the swishing of Monica's silk along the corridor. They stepped into the mirrored elevator. Ray stared at the floor and the tops of his navy brogue shoes. Monica was silent. It occurred to Ray that were he someone else, this would have been a perfect opportunity to talk to her, make a swift, smart comment that would break the ice and chip away at the amorphous, impenetrable impression he felt he had maintained, largely against his own will, ever since he had arrived at the branch. His fifty-fifth birthday had brought with it the first buds of peace with his own insularity, but the harsh winds of his own continual self-criticism had yet to completely subside.

The steel box shuddered gently as the unseen brakes clamped into place, ensuring they did not succumb to the endless pull of the earth. Lifting his head, Ray waited for Monica to step out of the elevator, ready to continue their two-person procession to the director's office, but Monica was standing still. With a nervous lurch of one of his organs, he realized she was staring straight at him.

"For what it's worth, Ray, I believe you."

Her tone was level, the pitch even. The deep, satin cadence of her voice, in which some nights Ray played his name over and over, carried no weight of emotion. He asked himself, as he walked in her shadow down the corridor a moment later, whether she had held his gaze a fraction longer than she ought.

The director was not in his office. The door was opened by a man in a double-breasted plum suit and what seemed to be cream alligator skin shoes.

"Mr. Blankenship, thank you for accepting our invitation." He smiled a glistening ivory smile and waved a hand toward the room, beckoning Ray in. Ray was acutely aware of the muffled footsteps his shoes made across the carpet as he followed the man's gesture into the center of the office.

"Ray, good to see you! You had a good weekend, yes?" Fielding, who gave no indication that he expected a response, was standing behind the director's desk, a large steel case open in front of him. From where he stood, Ray could not see its contents.

"Take a seat on the chair, will you, sport?" The plum-suited man was standing behind a large black leather chair positioned opposite the mahogany desk. His alabaster grin was still fixed firmly in place.

Ray sat down, casting a fleeting glance at Monica, who had her arms folded across her chest, one hand resting on the top of her bare forearm.

A sudden cold sting at his temple made Ray flinch. From behind him, Fielding's nameless colleague placed his hands on Ray's shoulders.

"Hold still, please, Mr. Blankenship, while I attach the sensors." Ray swallowed, the sandpapery insides of his throat scraping against one another.

"Can I ask what's going on?"

"You can indeed, Ray. After the most recent developments, we're just taking a few precautions. Need to make sure we know that everyone on the team is *on* the team, if you catch my drift." Fielding raised his head from the case and gave Ray a cheerful wink, the type Ray had only seen people do in movies. "Our friend here is just hooking you up to our fMRI. Why bother doing something when a machine can do it better, hey?"

Ray felt the bite of another steel sensor being stuck to his other temple. He had heard of this technique only in passing: the use of functional magnetic resonance imaging, more commonly known as fMRI, or in complete layman's terminology, brain imaging as a form of intentional deceit exposure. The technology had replaced the long-discredited polygraph method, which relied only on physiological indicators to assess a person's veracity; their blood pressure, respiratory rate, and the sweatiness of their palms. fMRI, on the other hand, measured changes in blood flow to determine which areas of the brain were being employed in the task at hand. In this case, truth telling, or the absence of it. Neurologically speaking, lies always started with a recollection of the truth, followed by a decision to conceal it, followed by the fabrication of an alternative narrative. Mendaciousness was more time and energy consuming than honesty.

Ray felt another cold nip at the crown of his head, followed by fingers adroitly foraging through his hair for the appertaining areas of his scalp, which would offer accurate readings of bodily functions over which he had no control. His skin itched. He searched for an inconspicuous, innocuous place to rest his eyes, deciding to join the dots on the tops of his shoes to distract him from the sensation of another man's skin against his own.

"There you go, Ray." He felt a heavy hand slap down on his shoulder and flinched again. "All thirty-six in place."

Ray nodded and attempted a smile.

"Once upon a time, we'd have had to put you in a big polo machine and sit behind a glass screen. Amazing how far technology's come, don't you think?" Fielding was looking not at Ray but at the large screen to which Ray's back was facing. He seemed to be tapping buttons in the steel case. Ray could taste spearmint and found himself wondering why it was that polo sweets had been discontinued. As a child, he had never liked them, considering any sweet that tastes like toothpaste to be a form of cruel adult deception.

Fielding passed the man in the alligator skin shoes a tablet. He in turn passed it to Ray.

"We're going to ask you to take a look at this tablet, Ray. All you need to do is follow any instructions we might give you." Fielding looked up at the screen behind Ray. "No need to worry, old sport—we haven't even begun yet." He flashed his insipid grin in Ray's direction, which did nothing to moderate the pulse Ray could feel quickening in his neck, which he was sure Fielding could see on the screen.

In the corner of the room, Ray heard Monica shift on her feet. Forgetting, in his concentration on ignoring the sensors being attached to him, that she had been there all along, he cast his gaze inadvertently over at her. She was concentrating on the wall behind Ray. Fielding looked down from the screen to Ray, sitting opposite him on the monstrous leather chair, and then followed his gaze over to Monica. His eyebrow raised almost imperceptibly, and Ray thought he saw something akin to amusement wash over the man's face.

Fielding seemed to be controlling the contents of the tablet from inside the steel case. He presented him first with a series of stock images that he asked Ray to describe; an apartment building, a basket of fruit (some of which Ray had not seen in over a decade), a child's drawing of an elephant, a black crow, and a topiary bush. Fielding's assistant seemed to be typing in figures from the large screen on his own handheld device. Ray assumed these depicted measures of his normal brain activity against which they could compare whatever was coming next.

"All right, Ray, if you could tell me the names of these people and your relationship with them." Fielding placed a heavy finger on a button, and a face appeared on the tablet before Ray.

It was his father. Ray swallowed, noting how the eyebrows of the familiar but forgotten face seemed to defy the effects of gravity.

"That's my father, Gerald." It felt strange to say his name. "He passed away just before the war."

"Just the name and relationship if you would, Ray," replied Fielding, who did not look away from the screen.

Ray looked back down at the tablet. The next face was Bosworth's. It occurred to Ray that had his father survived, he might be the same age as Bosworth was now.

"Bosworth, the concierge of my building."

Fielding nodded and typed something briskly into the keypad in front of him. The next face was Monica's secretary; Ray struggled to remember his name. This was followed by a copyist whose name Ray could also not recall. He was unsure whether or not he should be embarrassed at this fact.

Jill's face appeared next on the screen, followed by copyist 112's.

"Umm… Barney, he's a copyist in my division." A moment of gratitude toward Jill for mentioning his name washed over Ray, followed by a surge of unease. He wondered if they were both still being held for questioning.

Fielding turned to the other man, exchanging what must have been a meaningful glance for the assistant nodded and jotted down more notes.

The next face was the presiding head of Freedom Point, a woman named Felicity Harbinger, whom Ray had never met but whom he had always thought had a particularly distant look about her. A stream of faces followed, none of whom Ray recognized, but some of whom he thought he may have seen on the daily news broadcasts he watched over his evening coffee. The last face on the screen was Monica's. It must have been an old picture, because her hair was slightly longer and dyed a brick red.

Ray felt the skin of his cheeks prickle and hoped he had not blushed before he realized that even if he hadn't some signal would have registered on the screen behind him, and it would not have been a simple indication of recognition. The same expression passed over Fielding's face. He gestured with a tilt of his head to his assistant, who walked over to Monica and whispered something in a low voice, which Ray could not quite catch. Monica, who had tapped the screen of her tablet closed when he walked over, nodded to the man, her expression unchanging. Ray watched her leave.

When he returned to look at Fielding, he was met by what he was sure was a wider smile than usual, and something playing about the corners of the man's eyes.

"Doing all right there, Ray?"

Ray did not respond.

"I'd just like you to read the bits of text that appear on the screen and tell me where you've seen them before."

Time seemed to warp in the confines of the warm office. It must have been daylight outside, though Ray could not tell whether the weather was contributing to the heat within.

A part of his brain seemed to have decided to take its leave from the relentless asinine questioning and save him the cognitive cost of exhibiting his vexation. It chose a spot from his boyhood to explore, a hill behind his childhood home, under the outstretched branches of an oak tree that scribbled their shadows across the sky above him. Ray had spread out his coat and was lying on his back, an acorn cap on each of the fingers of his left hand that he was using to follow the lines of the latest sci-fi thriller his father had bought him. The sunlight, where it weaseled its way through the boughs, was hot on his bare calves and forearms. He remembered being hungry, but too engrossed in the plot to pick himself up and cycle down the hill toward home.

"This is an advert for ice alternatives." The reluctant part of Ray still in the room read out the familiar jingle, which he had often made efforts to deter from its insistence on replaying in his head at the most random moments of the day.

"And the next one?"

Ray read out the passage. "I think that's an excerpt from *Pulp Fiction*. Before one of the characters opens his suitcase."

"And do you recall what was in that suitcase, Ray?"

Ray thought hard. It had been several years since he'd rewatched the film, and he was surprised he even remembered the quotation. "No, I don't."

Fielding nodded. "And how about this one?"

For I say unto you, To every one that hath shall be given: but from him that hath not, even what he hath shall be taken away from him.

Ray felt the urge to scratch at his palm. He wondered what parts of his brain would light up at his resistance.

"That's a verse before one of the sections that went missing. It's a different version. But it's from the New Testament. From what I remember…"

Fielding's face remained stoic. His assistant scribbled something down.

By the time Ray was allowed to leave, his knees were sore from having been bent for so long, and his shoulders ached. He pulled off the steel sensors himself, politely declining any help, unable to bear the prospect of further intrusions into his personal space, internally or externally. He knew that his decision to leave work, rather than go back to his office, would be interpreted in the light of whatever results had been strewn across the screen behind him, but the irritation that had seized control of him seemed to fill every crevice the sensors were measuring. The walls of the lift seemed narrower, the air in the corridors suffocating. Without collecting his things from his office, he headed to the main reception and requested a transport pod home. His smartwatch beeped in protest to his change in schedule.

VII

When Ray returned to work the next morning, he found a message awaiting him on his desktop with a request for him to see Monica in her office. He steeled himself, determined not to let his heightened contempt toward Fielding, whom he presumed would also be present, take control of him.

His relief at finding Monica alone in her office was quickly replaced by a molten surge of discomfiture, which threatened to render him mute when Monica looked up at him. He cleared his throat.

"Your fMRI results were all clear, Ray. Nothing to worry about."

Ray nodded. He wondered whether Fielding had insisted she deliver this news, or whether she had.

"Have there been any developments?"

"No, nothing." Monica's brow furrowed. Expecting this to be the extent of the conversation, Ray turned one foot toward the door to leave. "It's strange. Three segments all disappear in the space of twenty-four hours the world over, and then nothing."

Ray straightened his feet. "Are they expecting any others to be deleted?"

"According to the information I've been given, Prognostications initially drew up several simulations, and based on the fact that there's been nothing since Friday, they all indicate that whatever message was being conveyed, these three segments must contain it."

"What's the message?"

"They're working on deciphering it."

"Something to do with violence?"

Ray suddenly noticed how tired Monica looked; the way her shoulders, usually pulled back, seemed to sag. He wondered whether it was her exhaustion that had led her to soften her usually brusque and parsimonious demeanor. As much as he thought now might be the time to bring her a coffee, ask if she'd had any sleep, he daren't stray anywhere other than the current direction of the conversation.

"It seems so. No indication of where it's from or who it's aimed at, though."

Ray was uncertain what to ask next that wouldn't involve stating the obvious. System checks of the highest level would have been run, codes analyzed down to each dash and period.

"It's not a virus?"

"It could be. It's not clear yet. It's no amateur attack, that's for sure."

"Clearly," Ray agreed.

"Security has been ramped up around the hard archives, too. And I need to ask you to keep an eye on the copy rooms. You'll need to report any anomalies to Feilding."

"Of course." He knew this meant the equivalent of spying on his department through use of the surfeit of surveillance cameras in almost every corner of the copy rooms.

"And…I'd appreciate it if you'd keep me in the loop, too." Monica was looking at him unwaveringly. Ray blinked, an unconscious attempt to break the eye contact that seemed to squeeze him from within.

"I'll make sure you're fully informed of anything I know."

Ray returned to his office surprisingly buoyant and logged into the surveillance systems. He swept the cameras around the room somewhat more enthusiastically than he could have anticipated.

~

Despite his scrupulous scrutiny of the copy rooms, his frequent checking of the flag reports, and his own scouring of the texts from which the segments had disappeared in the off chance the words may have reappeared, the next week passed uneventfully. Ray went to and from work in the travel pods from his usual hours of nine to five, returning to his soundless apartment every evening with nothing but mounting frustration at his inability to fulfill Monica's request.

Even his encounter with Laura Spinelli in the corridor, dressed in a silk slip far shorter than usual, did little to assuage his disappointment with the normality that seemed to have returned.

It was Bosworth in the end who broke the monotony. "I can't help noticing, sir," he said one evening as Ray waited for the elevator, "that you've seemed somewhat beat these past few evenings."

Ray turned abruptly toward the old man sitting behind his desk, wondering for a moment whether he was talking to someone else. The old man's eyes, Ray noticed, were heavily lidded, with layers of loose skin that seemed to blanket the watery gray irises beneath them.

"If I might be so bold, I'd venture to say I've seen that look before." The aqueous depths beneath the heavy lids seemed to twinkle in the soft light from his desk lamp.

"You have?" Ray was surprised that the man might ever have seen the likes of the weight he carried; the knowledge of a cyber-attack, the vanishing of ancient sacred texts, the exhaustion of interrogation, the burden of unfulfilled anticipation.

"Oh yes, sir. Woman trouble. It plays about the temples, you see." He gestured with a gnarled, arthritic finger to the thinning strands on either side of his forehead. Ray's cheeks flushed a sudden scarlet. He was not sure whether it was a reaction to the assertion that he had been exuding the air of a forlorn teenager or the fact that the old man seemed to have touched a nerve connected to a feeling he had never once openly expressed. He feigned as friendly a smile as he could muster.

"Your secret's safe with me, sir." The old man gave him a slow nod.

Ray nodded back.

~

Ray often wondered if his life had been as routine and calculated in the age before existence had been dominated by algorithms. It was hard to remember a time when the ethos of organization, meticulous habit, and cultivated customs had not been ingrained in him. As he heaved the grocery box onto his hip to press his finger to the keypad, he tried to remember back to when he was a child, to untangle the threads of his own volition from those of his parents, his teachers, all the adults around him who had imposed their own structures upon him.

Pushing open the apartment door with his knee, Ray set the box down on the kitchen counter and paused. With his eyes closed, in the quiet and familiarity that surrounded him, he took a series of deep breaths. His smartwatch beeped applaudingly. Ray set it to silent.

Regardless of whenever these habits had emerged, the knowledge of the familial comfort they brought him was enough for Ray. He engaged in them intimately.

On the low shelf, he straightened the shoes he had removed by the door, reaching for a wipe to polish away a smudge mark he had accumulated somewhere between work and home. Standing before the mirrored pane in his closet, he unknotted his cravat, red paisley with gold trim, and dropped it into the wicker basket ready for collection on Tuesday by the laundry service. He hung up his jacket, brushing the lapels to remove any dust, and hung the trousers over the bar of the hanger. His shirt he unbuttoned slowly, looking at his reflection. His smartwatch caught the light from the overhead lamp and glinted sharply in the mirror. He dropped the shirt into the basket too. His reflection tilted its head back at him, examining the figure before it. The dark, graying hair, almost all in place, the shadow of stubble emerging along his jawline, the bony shoulders and the wiry savannah of black and white hair strewn across his chest, funneling down toward his navel and disappearing beneath the light blue cotton underwear that fanned out around his long, narrow thighs. His red socks, matching the shade of his cravat, clung to his shins, and were beginning to sag around his ankles.

He stared at the shade. A fireman's red. The red of danger. Of warning. The red of the dots that had hovered over the map, indicating all the branches that had filed flags. The red of the line above Monica's eyes the morning he had stepped into her office.

Woman trouble. Ray's cheeks flushed again as he bent down quickly, pulled off his socks, and dumped them into the basket.

Dressed now in a matching pair of mint green pajamas, rimmed with emerald edging, Ray slid his feet into a pair of navy slippers and made his way to the kitchen.

Most accommodation was built with appliances that could produce tea or coffee at the click of a button, and indeed in the corner of the kitchen sat a large, highly polished steel coffeemaker. But Ray's had never been touched. He reached into the cabinet over the sink and pulled out a black ceramic jar with a gold lid. From it, he spooned a small heap of mock roasted coffee beans into a silver pot. From the drawer beneath the sink, he extracted a curved piece of metal with a round black handle. This he inserted into a hole at the side of the pot. Closing the lid, Ray began to turn the handle rhythmically. The beans inside crunched and burst, releasing their rich aroma, which wrapped itself around Ray in a soothing embrace. The resistance to the grinding slowly gave way to a steadier, softer motion, the teeth whirring smoothly as the beans reduced to a fine, velvety powder. Unscrewing the lid, Ray tipped the beans into the small compartment of a thick steel-bottomed percolator, filled the chamber below with filtered water from the fridge, and screwed the top on tight. He turned on the heat.

While water droplets crackled faintly against the induction pad beneath the pot, Ray carefully unpacked the contents of the grocery box. The fruit he lay in small basins in the sink, ready to disinfect. The packaging told him everything arrived washed and ready, but the years of contamination during the war and the heightened awareness of environmental pollutants that, although decreasing, had not yet been eradicated, had left him unable to eat anything fresh without first disinfecting it.

He placed the cartons of milk alternatives in the fridge, next to the cheese and butter substitutes. The elimination of meat from the global diet in an attempt to correct the damage done to the ecosystems, and to reduce the emission of greenhouse gasses by farm animals, and restore crops and grazing lands to forests, had also meant the absence of dairy from the supermarket shelves. This did not bother Ray as much as the scarcity of certain crops, including rice and wheat. Wheat harvests had been devastated by chemical attacks, and both grains had been hit hard by the droughts that continued to parch certain regions of the planet, rice in particular, which was grown in the saturated paddies of China, India, and other Southeast Asian lands, areas that had been hit hard by the war.

The bubbling of the percolator reached a throaty gargle just as Ray put away the last of the pre-packed meals. He turned off the stove and turned on the oven. Reaching back into the cupboard over the sink, he pulled down a small white porcelain cup and saucer, and set it on the counter. From a yellow tin, he took two thin ginger biscuits and propped them on the saucer next to the cup.

Pulling up the stool, he switched on the screen on the wall opposite to catch the evening news broadcast, seated himself comfortably at the counter, and, with a slow, deliberate trickle, poured out his coffee.

~

It was with some difficulty that Ray returned to his office after the briefing on Monday morning with instructions to return to work as usual. The firewalls that had been installed around the digital copies of all versions of the three sacred texts—the Tanakh, the New Testament, and the Quran—were impenetrable, Fielding informed Monica and Ray.

"We've had our best people on it. The window for any further attacks has most definitely been closed. We still have a team back at Prognostics trying to trace the hack and decipher the threat. But the simulations are not predicting even the remotest probability of a second wave of deletions. Monica, you've obviously ramped up security of the hard archives. They weren't the issue, but you know, best to cover all corners."

"We have. And we have set up a surveillance screen of the digital texts that will alert us if anything suspicious is detected." She tapped her pointer finger in the direction of the wall of what Fielding had assumed entirely as his headquarters away from home. Three large windows opened on the screen, each with a copy of the texts. She scrolled up and down each of them in turn with her finger.

"Perfect. Get the old machines to keep an eye on things." Fielding nodded enthusiastically, taking a loud slurp from his coffee cup.

"Ray, we'll need you to approve access to anyone still working on those files on an individual basis. But other than that, life returns to normal." Monica cast a rare, business-like smile in Ray's general direction. The weight she had been carrying seemed to have lifted, and the tightness around the corners of her mouth was fainter; her last hurdle left to surmount being the smooth departure of Fielding.

Ray took in the movements of the two people in the room with a dazed detachment. Monica was busy typing on her tablet, Fielding drinking his coffee while giving instructions to Monica's secretary via his earpiece on the documents to file before his leaving. Their figures seemed to swim before him, like the distorted visions of a patient sliding slowly under anesthetic. He swallowed.

"So…everything's back to normal?" He tried to bring the room into focus with his own voice.

"That's right," replied Monica, almost cheerfully, over her shoulder. Ray rose to his feet. His body felt heavy, as though being dragged into sleep. He blinked, as if fighting against the onset of unconsciousness.

The walk back to his office felt twice as long as usual, and by the time he reached the door he was exhausted and somewhat nauseated. He tried to recall what he had eaten for breakfast. The same thing he had eaten for breakfast for the past several years. Nothing about his morning had been out of the ordinary. Nothing about his life could possibly be out of the ordinary. The only hint, scent, trace of the extraordinary had been the discovery of the missing segments. He tried to recall the fear that had flooded him at the sight of the blank spaces on the scans of the ancient pages. He felt a ripple somewhere within him, but it was only a faint memory of a quickly fading feeling. Ray stared at his screen. His smartwatch beeped, bringing him back into the present.

He stared at it, then walked to the corner of the room, filled a thick mug with hot black coffee, and reluctantly opened his emails.

~

By three that afternoon, Ray had slipped back into the monotonous rhythms of his working life. He had cleared his overflowing inbox, addressed three management directives he'd had on his list for two weeks, and had initiated the transfer of a new shipment of books into the manuscript preparation department.

He was reading through the titles, with a forkful of lentil lasagna balanced at the corner of his mouth, when a sudden fervent pummeling at the door broke sharply through the silence, making him jump violently, spilling the food onto his thigh. He stood up quickly, half alarmed, half irritated at the spots of oil that had seeped into the fabric. His smartwatch was beeping wildly in protestation of his suddenly elevated heart rate.

"Come in," he called, just as a yellow-spectacled face flung open the door. The handle smashed into the hole that the copyist had left a week ago, about which Ray had neglected to inform the maintenance staff.

"Mr. Blankenship," huffed Monica's secretary. His face was red, and beads of sweat were pearled across his forehead and upper lip. He was wearing an acid-green shirt. Dark patches had formed under his arms. "Monica wants you immediately." He bent over, his hands on his knees. "She said to come to the surveillance room," he said, still talking to the floor.

Ray's mind raced with questions as he tried to stop himself from running the entire way down the corridor. Somewhere in the back of his mind, he was acutely aware that he did not want to arrive out of breath, nor did he want to raise further suspicions among anyone who had seen Monica's secretary loping along to his office.

Pausing before he reached the door, he collected himself, setting aside the resurgent flood of fear he had only that morning tried to recollect, and the inexplicable sensation of excitement, accompanied by a stomach-tugging sense of guilt. He put his hand on the doorknob and turned it.

The first face he saw was Fielding's. It was ashen. As though daubed in gray paint. He was staring at the screen, eyes fixed as though confronted by his own executioner. Monica stood next to him, tapping wildly in the direction of the wall, her arm outstretched. Neither of them looked at him. He followed their gaze toward the screen.

The three files that had been open when he had left—the Tanakh, the New Testament, and the Quran—each took up a third of the wall. They were going haywire, the text on each of them shooting frenziedly up and down the screen.

"What...?" His half-formed question hung in the fraught air, which seemed to crackle with a mixture of alarm and confusion, and Monica's frantic attempts to intervene in whatever was happening on the screen.

"It won't stop!" Her voice broke over the last syllable. Her eyes were wide.

The documents appeared to be scrolling wildly up and down, pausing fractionally, before reloading and jumping to another section.

Ray concentrated on the nearest, the New Testament, too distracted by the disjointed movements of the three together to determine what was happening. The scrolling paused momentarily. Ray was sure he saw the word *blood*. The document reloaded, flickering on the screen. And to his horror, he realized an entire verse had disappeared. The writing shot up the screen as the document scrolled through itself to a new section.

It paused again. Words flashed before them, jumping out of the page:

Lazy ...

gluttons...

evil...

At either side of the text, from the corners of his eyes, he could see the other documents thrashing up and down. Ray watched the edges of the document shudder as it reloaded. Another verse vanished.

Ray felt himself stung into action. He rounded the desktop, tapping violently on its smooth surface, trying to find anything that might override the system, or at least end the program. He looked back up at the texts on the walls. Scrolling. Pausing. Reloading. Words flashing.

Beating...

My master...

servants...

drunk...

Then they disappeared. Replaced only by a blank space between the streams of writing above and below that flashed briefly like a streak of lightning across the page before the manic scrolling resumed.

Ray's eyes moved to the adjacent document–the Tanakh. The writing flailed up and down the screen before him. The same thing was happening

uproar...

nations massing...

an army...   *war...*

Pause. Reload. Vanish. Scroll. Stop. Words shimmered again on the page.

idols...

gods...

Fight...

attack...

the sword...   *burned down their city...*

no one to rescue them

Then an entire section was wiped. He swept his eyes across to the furthest text. The Quran. He had caught it just as the screen hovered at a page. His eyes darted back and forth, pulling words from the page, the sweat on his neck cold, his throat dry, his heart racing.

smite their necks...

make them prisoners...

ransom...

The page reloaded. The blank space appeared. The rapid scrolling continued. Verses flashed before them. A furor of black shapes and cream pages, blurring into a gray haze, until it came abruptly to a stop. The page shuddered; words reached out and snatched their glances.

cast horror…

evil doers…

fire will be their home.

And then, with a convulsion of the screen, yet another verse was gone.

Ray opened the system settings, pulled up the security software. The projection on the wall seemed entirely disconnected from the desktop. He frantically tried to activate the system reset, but it required permissions from the director, and stubbornly insisted that his access was denied.

"It's no use." Fielding's voice was flat and gravelly, as though it had difficulty coming out of his throat. "We've been hijacked."

A shiver ran up Ray's forearms, dragging the hairs on his skin upright. He suddenly felt freezing cold. He looked up at the screen.

Scroll. Pause. Reload. Delete.
Scroll. Pause. Reload. Delete.
Scroll. Pause. Reload. Delete.

By the time the screens slowed, and reloaded themselves for the final time, seven minutes had passed. To each of the three standing in the room, it had felt like a century. Red lights pulsed in all corners of the screen, illuminating the office in a bloody haze, and an incessant wailing that Ray had not noticed before was coming from the inbuilt speakers in the corners of the room.

"Can someone stop that fucking noise!" Fielding, as though suddenly rediscovering his ability to move, slammed his hand down on the corner of the desk.

The wailing stopped abruptly. It occurred to Ray that the silence that replaced it was far eerier. It seemed to amplify the frozen screens that lay mutilated across the wall before them.

Monica, realizing she once again had control of the desktop system though not yet the screen, ran the diagnostics tool on each of the documents. Fielding grunted. Breathing heavily, he rummaged around in his jacket for his earpieces. He shoved them into his ears and pulled open the door. Ray could hear him clear his throat loudly as he connected to someone on the other end of the line.

The beeping of the diagnostics tool on the desktop cut sharply through the silence, telling them it had calculated the percentage of remaining text. Monica's eyes flitted quickly across the screen. She slumped down heavily in her chair and ran a hand over her forehead.

"What's the damage?" Ray could feel a cold sheen of sweat on his palms and at the back of his neck.

Monica looked up at him; the lines above her eyes were a dark gray. "We've lost thirty-five percent."

Ray stared at her. She looked from him to the screen. The pulsing red light caught in her pupils.

"If this keeps happening, there'll be nothing left…"

PART II

I

Ray had chosen not to incline his passenger seat to its horizontal position. He was sure he would not be able to sleep. He looked instead out of the thick reinforced glass windows, de-tinted now that night had fallen, at the shadowy landscape tearing past. The cities the bullet train had cut through had thinned into fields of solar panels, their darkened tilted plates glinting with the reflection of the lights from the passenger windows.

Ray was glad he had been allocated a seat facing the back of the train, preferring to see the world receding from him, rather than facing the accelerated onslaught of the unknown.

He had never traveled by bullet train. He'd never had cause to. There was nothing beyond the reaches of his small spot in Zone 4 that he could not see in high-definition digital format. The appeal of new places and unfamiliar settings had long lost its glitter. The rapid changes that years of conflict had precipitated, followed by the gargantuan efforts to rebuild, renew, and rejuvenate what was damaged and destroyed, had made what had once been home often feel like a foreign land. Ray rarely strayed from his well-worn route, from home to the office, and from office to home, all via transport pod, slathered in quick-absorbing SPF creams to protect his skin from the harmful effects of the high UV levels and bedecked in dark glasses to stave off the onset of cataracts and macular degeneration in the brief moments he stepped into direct sunlight.

On the rare and calculated occasions that he ventured out to the mall complexes, designed to fill the gaps in the consumer experience that the online purchasing systems had yet to plug—the ability to lift a fruit and inhale its perfume, the feel of silk between one's fingers—he would quickly come to regret these detours from the ordinary, and it would take all his known reserves of staying power not to turn and head for the nearest exit.

This made Ray the perfect candidate for predictability. He was sure comparatively few algorithms lay behind the beeping of his smartwatch, the advertisements that appeared when he turned on his home desktop system, and the suggestions his subscription services proffered on a regular basis. It made the calculation of his departure date, the year his body would eventually have deteriorated beyond further use, straightforward.

The number of years determined by his genetic code and health heritage minus the impact of environmental factors; diet, smoking, alcohol consumption, exposure to direct sunlight, stress levels, exercise, profession, and marital status. If these were controlled and physicians' guidelines were followed, there would be no reason Ray would not complete his full lifespan. The only other possible interference were accidents and what were once, in an era of paper and overpopulation, known as "acts of God." This term had long been removed from legal documentation. Legal firms argued that its inclusion was discriminatory against non-theist populations, and that the terminology was out of sync with a world in which the rigors of science, not divinity, underlay explanations.

Those of a more cynical persuasion did not share the fact that the removal of this phrase in a world in which freak weather and environmental conniptions were not uncommon meant that insurance firms drastically reduced their number of payouts. Ray suspected that if he checked the notifications that he had silenced on his smartwatch, they would tell him precisely the toll that his recent increased stress levels would have on the eighty-four years carved out as his niche on earth.

He wondered, as he often did when meeting a new person, which was not often, how long the woman sitting opposite him had left. She had also chosen not to recline her passenger seat. Her head was tipped slightly back against the headrest, and her eyes were closed. If he focused, Ray could see her reflection in the thick glass. Her chest rose and fell slowly. The long, thick hair, the color of wine, draped over her shoulders, shifted slightly with each breath. She had to be at least forty, Ray determined. Less on account of her appearance, and more based on the fact that it was so rare to encounter anyone younger than thirty in the post-war world.

A sudden sharp fullness behind his eardrums alerted Ray to the fact that they had just entered a tunnel. The woman's reflection became interrupted by the intermittent lights inlaid into the dark walls. Her image played on the glass like an old black and white movie, flickering. Her lips were thin, the same color as her hair. Her cupid's bow was pulled taut, making the two lines leading to her nostrils distinctly pronounced. The jacket that she had pulled over her chest had slipped down, revealing the collar of a white sleeveless satin shirt, a thin gold chain around her neck, and the tops of her shoulders. Allegra Akihiro, she had introduced herself as, shaking his hand firmly as they'd stood in the train station. Expert in sacred manuscripts and historiography.

Unnerved and comforted in equal measure at the thought of not traveling alone to Freedom Point, Ray had steeled himself for conversation. But Allegra had simply nodded to him once he sat down, pulled her jacket over her, and closed her eyes.

If she were forty, the maximum reasonable remaining amount that could be expected before her departure was sixty years. With the vast strides the medical profession had made in the treatment of terminal diseases, centenarians were predicted to be far more common in the next thirty to fifty years. The global pandemics that had crippled even the wealthiest of nations in the '20s had led to a relaxation of licensing laws and spurred pharmacologists to explore new avenues for inoculation against diseases. It was unlikely, therefore, that the woman sitting opposite him would die of any serious health condition. It was more likely that they would both die in a train crash. The odds were small, available mandatorily on the company website. And no adverse weather conditions or technical malfunctions had been detected. This train would run smoothly. By all accounts and predictions, Ray would live to eighty-four.

The tinkle of a teacup in a saucer coaxed Ray back into consciousness. He had fallen asleep with his head against the window, his breath making billowing patches of condensation on the now tinted panes. He sat up slowly, one hand on his neck to stymie the ache that stretched from his ear to his shoulder and cleared his throat.

"Coffee, Mr. Blankenship?"

The woman standing over him, coffeepot poised over his cup, had a distinctly familiar feel about her. Ray struggled to identify why, in the same moment that he registered the smell of coffee wafting over him.

"Yes, thank you, black." He looked up at her, uncomfortable with this level of human proximity upon awakening.

"Of course, sir," she smiled cheerfully, pouring out a thin stream of glistening brown liquid from the bright yellow pot.

The distinct air of the woman opposite him slowly swam into Ray's awareness beyond the cascading rivulet of coffee. Only her eyes were visible over the rim of her cup. Ray ran his finger around his cravat, which had stuck to his neck during his sleep.

Lowering her cup back into its saucer and setting it neatly on the large table between them, the woman opposite looked up at Ray.

"Good morning." Though the corners of lips moved only slightly, her face seemed to smile. For the first time since they had shaken hands at the station, Ray noticed her eyes were almost black.

"The buffet is ready in the food carriage," the stewardess's voice chimed, not dissimilar to the tinkling of the teacups on the cart. Ray watched her push it through the doors at the end of their carriage.

"I've heard the breakfasts on the Freedom Express are exceptional." Standing, Allegra whirled her jacket deftly around her shoulders, and brushed past him. Ray thought he caught the scent of almonds.

The buffet carriage was twice the length of a normal passenger carriage. Stepping through the sliding doors after Allegra, Ray was welcomed by a gust of richly aromaed air.

"Breakfast" had been a misnomer. The countertops that protruded from the walls heaved with every possible style of dish. Ray steadied himself for a moment, heady from the scents and the hangover of sleep. Allegra was already making her way swiftly down the aisle, a finger trailing through the air as though she were conducting her menu as she walked.

Ray paused, turning to the wide counter to his left, banked high with pastries. Their rich golden flakes, blossoming with jams of different colors, were identified by the inconspicuous digital descriptions beneath the edge of each plate. Speckled fig jams, gleaming pineapple, crimson pomegranate preserve, blueberry and elderflower, ginger and orange, rose and raspberry. It occurred to Ray that if ever real fruits might continue to exist—fruits that had struggled during the droughts and disappeared from supermarket shelves—the Freedom

Express would be one of the only places likely to have them. He lifted a fragrant lemon pastry with a vibrant set of tongs, examining it. It would be impossible to tell whether or not these were simply substitutes like the rest of the population was used to. The built-in screen on the wall above invited passengers to tap to view ingredients and allergens, but Ray decided against testing his theory.

A tray emerged from a slot in the counter, gleaming silver cutlery embedded in a groove at one side. He put the pastry on a plate and set it on the tray.

The mound of steaming scrambled eggs, freckled with pepper and chives, did not surprise him. In the age of substitutes, egg alternatives, fine yellow powders used for baking and scrambling were common, but he was surprised to see a pile of what looked like fried eggs on a large bright blue porcelain platter sitting next to them, their edges crispy, the color of caramel, their yolks burnished, reflecting the overhead lights. Ray resisted the urge to prod one with the tongs and continued his way down the counters, driven more now by curiosity than hunger. Discreetly, he examined the heaps of fried mushrooms and small hills of bacon, which he could not help but poke discreetly with a fork, as well as the stacks of fluffy pancakes and assortments of crepes, stuffed with everything from salmon and cream cheese to chocolate.

He reached a new counter. Set within the countertop were large, colorful metal lids, each with a raised mechanism in the middle. The screen over the counter showed a widely smiling young man demonstrating how to fill a bowl with soup. Ray read the descriptions. Peanut and sweet potato; kale, butter bean, and miso broth; tomato, red pepper, and paprika; wonton soup; gazpacho; lobster bisque; clam chowder.

By now, Ray was sure that at least some of the ingredients must be substitutes. He recalled the legislation that banned the consumption of lobsters upon the discovery that they, along with octopi and other crustaceans, were sentient beings capable of feeling pain. He took a bowl and placed it on top of a copper-colored lid. A small circle in the bottom of the bowl clicked into place, revealing a series of knife-thin slits. A crystal swirl of clear, golden consommé poured in. A savory meaty steam floated up into Ray's nostrils. He reached for a crusty bread roll from the baskets next to the soups. Detaching his bowl from the mechanism, he balanced this on his tray next to the pastry and carried on his perusal of the counters. Rice of various flavors and descriptions, fried with eggs, with beans, with dill, with saffron, sat next to containers of stews and sauces that all fought with each other for prominence in the orchestra of scents that surrounded them.

What interested Ray most were the vegetables. It was easy, he knew, to disguise substitutes in soups and stews, but producing substitutes with the shapes and textures of rare and extinct vegetables seemed too far-fetched for even the most modern manufacturing methods. By the time Ray returned to his seat, his tray was piled high with a bizarre, eclectic, and hopeful combination of foods. Next to his pastry and his soup sat a plate of thinly sliced avocado, a small bowl of plump strawberries, a fried egg that he had returned for, a prawn cocktail—the pink shrimp hanging daintily over the sides of an ornate glass—a stick of satay chicken strips, a pile of crispy spring rolls, a small pot of Greek yogurt topped with thick, treacly honey, and a bowl of sweet potato and sage gnocchi that had refused to let him pass without it.

Ray bit into a firm, juicy shrimp, feeling his teeth cut through the meaty flesh. Indistinct memories of boyhood swam around the peripheries of his vision. He dipped the remainder into the Marie Rose sauce and popped it into his mouth.

Allegra emerged from the doors behind him and took her seat opposite. She set down her tray. With the deft movements of a chess player, she maneuvered the small bowls and plates into a neat arrangement. Apparently pleased with the organized array before her, she closed her eyes, a fraction longer than a blink. In the breath she exhaled, her shoulders falling, she seemed to collect stray corners of herself, smoothing out her own edges, until she had recomposed herself into a formidably solid form.

She looked up at Ray. "Bon Appetit," she said, toasting him with a forkful of bright, glistening fruit.

~

"Can I take your tray, sir?"

The tinkling voice startled him. Ray raised his gaze from his tablet to the stewardess standing neatly next to their table. Hastily piling on vagrant cutlery and napkins, he nodded, fumbling with his awkward attempts to make her job easier for her.

"I can do that. Thank you, sir." Her smile brought back once again the uneasy feeling of forgotten familiarity. He felt Allegra's discreet attention on him, which only exacerbated his quiet distress.

The woman reached for a fork that had migrated to the far end of the table. As she stretched her fingers, her wrist slid out from the coral-colored sleeve of her uniform, and Ray caught sight of the faint indent, lit by the fragile glow of an inner LED.

He looked up sharply at her face, scanning it swiftly. At first, he assumed he had simply missed the signs because he seldom looked at people if they were looking at him. But one could always tell by the ears.

Only humans had ear canals. Only humans needed them. In companions, ear canals were liabilities, spaces into which small things could get lost, too likely to be overlooked in the disinfection process, too close to the internal wiring. They received audio input instead via small microphones implanted behind the ear. But the dark, fleshy duct in the model before him plunged deep into the silicone head. Ray felt a repulsive, almost inescapable urge to feel how far it went.

The buzzing of his tablet distracted him from his discomfort. An encrypted message. His face scan unlocked the screen in an instant. Three further security checks were required to download a message of this type. He entered his password, placed his index fingertip on the scanner, and held the tablet up to his face to scan his retina. The tablet buzzed, confirming his identity.

It took two readings of the message from Fielding for Ray to understand what had happened. Not because Fielding had not been clear. His tone was direct, his wording sparse. But because Ray could not quite believe what he was reading:

Every digital secondary document containing the verses that had disappeared had been wiped. In their entirety.

Millions of books of exegesis, explanations, speeches, and sermons had been corrupted. Where they could be opened, only blank pages were proffered. The epidemic of erasure did not end with exegesis. Apocrypha, extra-Biblical words that had never made it into the accepted canon, pseudepigrapha, later Jewish writings ascribed to prophets and patriarchs, books of jurisprudence, even history; a total of over a million titles had, overnight, been plagued with whatever virus was eating through them.

Ray read the message again, just to be sure. Did this mean that the primary texts still existed, at least in part? With a series of taps, and another series of identity scans, imposed as part of the security clamp-down, he logged into his work desktop and pulled up the disfigured texts that still flashed wildly before him when he closed his eyes. He had understood correctly. They were still accessible, and what was left of the primary texts was still in place.

He sat back in his seat, and noticed that Allegra, too, had been reading from her tablet. She pushed it away from her, sliding it across the table as though in an attempt to examine from a distance the information Ray presumed she had also just received.

The train was lit with the anemic stream of filtered light through the tinted windows. It bathed the carriage in sepia tones, offset by the lights that shone on them discreetly overhead, supplementing the sunlight. A sudden wave of fatigue washed over him.

"You know what I find interesting?" Allegra's voice snatched Ray out of his languor. She did not seem to be looking directly at him, rather toward him. "Is that with all our technology, our algorithmic fortresses, we still have not managed to protect ourselves from a repeat of the sacking of Baghdad."

Allegra had spotted the stewardess and had gestured smilingly for some coffee. Ray tilted his head, confused as to what the now uninhabited capital of what was once Iraq might have to do with a cyber-attack.

"The sacking of Baghdad," he repeated, afraid that if he posed it as a question he might come across as ignorant.

Allegra returned her gaze to his general direction. "Mmm…" she confirmed. "1258. The Mongols descend on the city like a scourge. Those who tried to negotiate with Hulagu, the sanguinary leader of the incipient steppe empire, were murdered. The city was depopulated, much like it was during the war of '33. But perhaps the most extreme violence that was wrought was not upon the people, but the libraries. Baghdad had been a seat of knowledge. But after the Mongol siege, the streets ran red with blood, and the Tigris ran black with ink. Books were torn from their covers, the leather turned into soldiers' sandals who trampled pages into the mud. But it was not just libraries that were destroyed. The jewel in Baghdad's crown, its *piece de la resistance*, was none other than the House of Wisdom."

She paused to allow the stewardess to refill her coffee cup. Ray watched her fingertips as she held the rim.

"Liquid black gold," she said, raising the cup in Ray's direction, cradling the saucer in her other hand below it. She took an appreciative sip. "The House of Wisdom was the Grand Library of Baghdad, founded in the eighth century. You have to imagine it. Scholars flocking from all corners of the globe, bringing with them their ideas, their challenges, their questions to consult the wealth of information stored in its walls. Scouts sent out in search of rare and ancient manuscripts, tome upon tome of unique and innovative works. Shelves bursting with everything the world knew about itself. An academy of thought, of poetry, of literature, of science. The House of Wisdom, one of the great wonders of the world, was burned. Razed to the ground. Gutted of its contents by the unlettered."

Allegra, enraptured with the picture she herself was describing, leaned forward, setting down her cup with a clink. "Ignorance has always been the greatest enemy to progress."

"Do you think that's what's happening now? An attack? By…" Ray hesitated to give a name to what might lurk in the shadows.

"It's not my job to identify *who*; it's my job to identify *what*. What is going on, what is disappearing, what might be being communicated? It's just the irony that strikes me. With all its defenses, Baghdad, once the seat of one of the world's most powerful empire, was ransacked. With all our defenses, our libraries may be ransacked too. We still haven't figured out how to stop it."

She waved again at the stewardess, who Ray realized must be hovering somewhere behind him at the back of the carriage.

"He needs some more coffee." Allegra gestured to Ray. Despite himself, he smiled.

II

Freedom Point was built in a hurry. That much was evident from the unexpected amount of solid, cold concrete.

The gnarly edges of the station sidewalk onto which Ray alighted, though slathered in thick, colorful paint, spoke to the speed with which they had been laid. It was only upon arrival that Ray realized he had imagined a city of glass.

An abrasively friendly pod operator, dressed in a portly royal blue uniform, shepherded them through the crowd of people who had bled out from the train and into their designated transport pod parked underground.

"No tinted windows here!" he chirped from the front seat, as they zipped out of the vast maze of underground levels and crept out behind a slow stream of pods into the glare. Ray blinked, squintingly. Allegra shaded her eyes.

"You can open your window if you like. We lie here under the protection of the almighty dome!" The operator chuckled.

Ray glanced over at Allegra, who had already pressed her finger into the groove to lower the glass. A rush of balmy air swept in.

"How do you keep it climate controlled?" Allegra was leaning forward asking the operator.

"Oh, there's all sorts of technology they've got going on here. It's mostly tidal powered." He settled down into his seat, one hand comfortably on the now automated controls, a remnant from the days of manual driving. Chauffeurs and operators were now only really safety mechanisms for instances of emergencies, much like train drivers had once been, less driving than managing the vehicle.

"The almighty dome," he chuckled again, "reaches right out into the ocean about five miles from the shore. And it's anchored into the seabed by these pillars." He gesticulated widely with his arms to demonstrate their girth. "And between each pillar are dynamos... I think that's the name... Anyhow, machines that harvest the wave energy. They allow the waves to come to shore, but at least half the energy of the tides goes into powering these machines. That, and power from the solar fields."

Ray, who had now opened his window too, leaned his head just beyond the outer edge of the pod. The breeze battered him with breathy gulps.

They were driving down the outer lane of a vast highway. Ray counted at least eleven lanes, each with brightly colored pods buzzing past, like iridescent insects. Squinting, he looked skywards. What he had expected to see, he was not sure. What met him, when he adjusted to the eye-watering amount of light that flooded his pupils, was little more than a summer haze. A nondescript endlessness, devoid of color, texture, even depth. Ray felt the backs of his eyes begin to ache, and he drew his head back into the pod.

The operator was still offering his theatrical explanations of the infrastructure of Freedom Point to Allegra, who peppered his performance with sporadic interjections.

Ray turned his attention to the views speeding past. The conveyor-belt of pods came to an abrupt halt as buildings slammed into view. A jungled mass of concrete and steel.

The pod had reduced its speed, and there was a momentary lull in the operator's commentary as he turned to check the controls. Buildings swept up either side of them; gray, stark, smooth from this distance. Unimaginative in their architecture, remarkably dull. Facades of stone, studded with rows of windows, as though each building was a table waiting to be filled with figures, ready to be summed and totaled.

A streak of color whipped past, an alarming vein of green in the spread of stone. An enormous banner was draped down the front of a building, words splashed across it in a vibrant yellow: "The Color Initiative: Make a Splash!"

Next a deep purple banner, then a cerulean blue one. Technicolor streams sliced through the current of concrete, increasing in frequency as they drove deeper toward the heart of the city. People scurried along the sidewalks, dressed in an eclectic array of colors and fabrics, busy, preoccupied. Some rode scooters that whined along next to the pods, weaving in and out of traffic, the bright round helmets of their riders making them look like bowling pins.

The thicket of buildings slowly thinned, giving way to colossal steel towers, connected by highway-breadth bridges, climbing up like a stiff, three-dimensional ladder of steel DNA; the office buildings of which Ray had heard only rumors, as wide as city blocks, that disappeared into a point somewhere above them. From their sides cascaded thick, iron-wrought supports that burrowed miles into the ground beneath them, so that everywhere one looked, their view was dissected by dark, diagonal lines. They crisscrossed above the road, like permanent comet streaks, almost audible as the small pod drove beneath them. The city block colossi themselves, it appeared, acted somewhat like tent poles, holding aloft the unseen, all-protecting dome miles above the center at which lay the buildings of Freedom Parliament.

"To stop the sky from falling." Allegra was leaning out of her window, gazing up.

Someone, undoubtedly buried deep in an advertising department somewhere, had had the bright idea of rigging digital billboards to each of these arachnidite structures. In crisp definition, advertisements for fitness programs, Vitamix supplements, sperm donation, live-in companions, and government family starter support packs shone down from above them.

"Start your Freedom Family today!" beamed an airbrushed couple looking down at a gurgling babe in a rainbow crib. "Guaranteed housing, schooling, and live-in support so you can contribute to the growth of the global nation!" More incandescent smiles.

At the foot of each of the towers were gardens; wide-open spaces of lush green, oases of foliage pooled around the gargantuan metal palms. Trees, dwarfed by the towers, shaded benches upon which people had gathered for their lunch. The pod slowed to a halt at the corner beneath a large stop sign.

"This is as far as I can take you," apologized the operator. "No vehicles allowed in Freedom Point center. Security precautions." He nodded wisely.

The Department of Prognostication was located in the last tower at the edge of the city's heart. Ray struggled to recall the last time he had walked outside further than fifty feet during daylight hours. He reached instinctively for his pocket-sized tube of SPF. Gingerly, he stepped out of the pod, blinking in the direct exposure now to the brightness that surrounded him.

Following the operator's directions, superfluous since large, bold street signs littered every corner, he and Allegra made their way along the street toward the city center, following the flame orange signs for the building's entrance.

Having dismantled his perceptions of the global capital as a shiny, futuristic hub of sophistication on arrival, as they approached the center of Freedom Point, Ray was forced to reconstruct this image, at least in part. The Houses of Parliament, which now emerged around the corner, were circular, tapering up gradually at first from a wide base, then narrowing dramatically toward a sharp, towering peak that glinted like a giant needle. The walls of the building, those that could be seen, were painted entirely white. The rest of the exterior was covered in vast glass tubes that wound their way up the building, and through which Ray realized he could see people walking. Large letters were set in stone into the grass bank around it:

Welcome to Freedom Point.
Hub of Peace, Liberty, and Stability.

Huge flags the size of small lakes fluttered in the artificial breeze in a ring around the building, lapping at the air around them. Ray stopped, looking from the brutality of the towering monstrosity of the steel building to his left, to the glittering face of the building that swirled up from the ground, an inverted vortex. Allegra, who had walked on toward the entrance, suddenly registered his absence, and turned back to draw him out of his reverie.

"It's a wonder why humans can't learn from nature how to create things of beauty." She put a hand on his elbow. "Come on, we'll be late."

The Department of Prognostication, they discovered, looking around for the signs, was located behind the third entrance in the vast building to their left. They climbed the studded steel steps to the gaping doors over which the name of the department stood in harsh iron letters.

A bored voice droned through the speakers embedded in the doorframe: "Scan your chips, please." Ray and Allegra swiped their fingers over the sensor pads above the door handles. "Face the camera."

The doors swung heavily inwards into a large, pale green foyer, dotted with large, drooping aspidistras, which gave Ray the fleeting feeling of walking into his childhood dentist clinic. They walked over to a receptionist, typing with severe concentration behind a looming desk, his back militarily straight, and his fingers hammering out a concerto of clicks on his desktop. The parting in his fluorescent pink hair was razor-edged. He turned his stodgy face toward them, revealing a waxy mustache of almost the same hue. He looked annoyed to see them.

"Yes?"

"We're here to see Mr. Marshal Fielding," Allegra said with a smile that seemed to tell him that while she could understand he was busy there was really no need to be rude.

The receptionist shifted his shoulders and looked back at his screen.

"Can I have your names?" He turned back to Allegra, whose expression had not altered. "Please." His Adam's apple bobbed in his throat.

Ray examined the small digital screen of the lanyard draped around his neck, avoiding his reflection in the lift mirror as they ascended to Fielding's office on the 356th floor. The lift, given the soaring height of the building, was fitted with benches covered in a thick pistachio-colored fabric, with the department logo, a jagged line ending in an arrowhead, woven into the design. Allegra had taken a seat on the bench and was scrolling through various charts and diagrams on her tablet, her thick, silky hair clipped back away from her face with a thin jade clasp.

Ray ran his finger around the edge of his cravat and stole a glance in the mirror to straighten it. The peacock blue and gold pattern matched the brilliant hue of his socks and stood out elegantly against the navy tweed of his suit. The blue did little to inspire the tranquility the Color Initiative adverts promised.

He knew he was there to advise on the workings of the various Literature Hub branches, the ins and outs of their digitization, cataloging, and security systems, though what use this would be in the face of a cyber enemy already able to burn through some of the most sophisticated firewalls in existence he did not know. He wondered whether his invitation was less an attempt to involve him, and more an attempt to keep an eye on him, as the first person to have raised the flag. Though at this point such fears were completely irrational, it did not stop Ray from running through multiple interrogation scenarios and wondering who would replace him if he were thrown into one of the offshore jails.

"Ray, my old pal!" boomed Fielding's voice, far too soon after the elevator doors had opened. Clapping a heavy hand on Ray's back, Fielding pumped his other hand up and down with piston-like force. "And you must be Miss Akihiro, our specialist brainbox." He put his spade-sized hand out toward Allegra.

"It's Dr. Akihiro, actually," she said, with a similar smile to the one she'd given to the receptionist.

Fielding gave Ray a knowing nod, tilting his head toward her. "Doc it is!"

"Now," he continued, striding toward the door of a large meeting room to which he'd lead them. Like an avalanche, his smile fell from his face, revealing a sudden seriousness, as though he no longer deemed his own exuberance appropriate. "Time to talk business."

Swiping his finger against the sensor, Fielding pushed the door open to reveal a room of similarly unsmiling faces, dressed in an array of garish suits. They turned, like a parliament of gaudy owls, their heads swiveling to stare at the newcomers. Fielding waved them to a seat at the edge of the large desktop.

"Welcome to the Investigation Committee. Committee, this is Ray Blankenship, head archivist at the Zone 4 branch and the first one to discover the deletion." Ray was met with nods, which he returned. "And *Dr*.," Fielding continued, leaning heavily into the stress on her title, "Allegra Akihiro, resident Literature Hub scholar and specialist in…" He picked up his tablet to examine her full title. "…sacred manuscripts and historiography."

Heads bobbed once again.

"As you all know, the Lit Hub's soft archives have recently been hit by a wave of cyber-attacks of a type unseen since the spate of digital hostilities in '35. Initially, three targets were hit. Segments a, b, and c." He waved his arm in the direction of the wall behind him, upon which three pages had appeared in crisp definition, the gashes of blank space running across each.

"We can't provide you with the text digitally since, given the nature of this attack, digitizations of the text are automatically corrupted. But Dr. Akihiro, I'm sure, can fill you in on the contents."

Ray's palms itched. He was suddenly parched. Breakfast seemed like months ago. His smartwatch buzzed with a low vibration. He glanced at the screen and fumbled with the controls to silence it.

As if in response to his own thirst, the middle of the large, shiny, white glass desktop around which they were sitting opened up and a large tray of silver tea and coffeepots, glass jugs of intensely colored juices, and emerald bottles of sparkling water rose steadily. Ray eyed them discreetly.

"Since then, despite robust upgrades to the security systems in place, two further attacks have been launched. The first targeted these primary texts." Fielding's eyes flitted back to his tablet. "The Old and New Testaments and the Quran, the main texts of three religions, each with dwindling numbers of followers. Approximately thirty-five percent of the contents of each were targeted and all traces of their online presence has disappeared. That goes for scans of the originals in all languages, as well as any record of them in supplementary texts, plus all and any text copies online." Fielding exhaled deeply through his nose as though this had somehow been a personal attack.

"What we might once have referred to as 'military grade' security was put in place, and for a week this seemed to have staved off any attacks. However, just this morning, a third offensive was launched, and it seems that all supplementary texts relating to any of the missing segments were corrupted or removed. They are no longer digitally accessible."

Fielding placed both his hands on the edge of the desktop and leaned forward.

"Ladies and gentlemen, we may be facing a renewed cultural terrorism offensive. Granted, this is an unusual target given the…irrelevance of these texts." He gestured, as though batting away a fly. "Nevertheless, it highlights a breach in our systems and an intentional attack on our attempts to digitize the printed word for prognostication purposes. And an attack against predictions is an attack against our way of life." His jaw was set firmly, accentuating its jutting edges.

From the corner of his eye, Ray noticed a woman reach forward and pour herself a cup of coffee.

"Now…" Fielding stood up straight again, running a hand through his hair. "…our job here is to predict what will be targeted next, so we can beat these bastards to it." He slammed his fist into his open palm. "Which brings me to our guests here. We have launched a two-pronged counterattack strategy. The first is to move all the soft archives to the Freedom Point network, where it will be secured under the most advanced systems this planet has ever seen. That's where you come in, Ray.

We'll need your expertise in ensuring nothing is lost in the cataloging process. We'll come back to that later.

"More pressingly, as far as you are all concerned, is the prognostics dimension to this, which is the second canon in our arsenal, so to speak. Dr. Akihiro, I know you've been looking at the data behind the attacks. Tell us what you know."

Fielding maneuvered into the wide, empty chair at the head of the table, swiping up a bottle of sparkling water, which he unscrewed and took a long swig from. Ray slid one toward himself along the desktop and filled a glass. He disliked the metallic taste and the sharp bite of sparkling water, but he was too thirsty to care. He took three grateful sips.

"Thank you, Mr. Fielding." Allegra reached down toward the leather bag she had leaned against her chair, pulling out a sheaf of papers. "Last week, I commissioned a team at the research branch to transcribe the missing verses onto paper. Unusual, yes, given the technology at our fingertips, but as Mr. Fielding has informed us, any attempt to upload, type, or scan these sections digitally resulted in their immediate erasure." She handed the pile to Ray. "Do take a look and pass them around."

Ray felt the smooth, velvety sheets against his fingertips, and the whispering as they slid apart from each other.

"As you may notice, there is a theme to these verses, and…" She swept her finger against the desktop, bringing up the screen she had been reading on her tablet. "…certain keywords are recurrent."

The words in their black fonts stood out in stark contrast to the gleaming white of the screen; words Ray recognized from the screens that had thrashed angrily back in the office.

Kill
Fight

Blood
Slay

"We've calculated the frequencies of these words and run a series of content analyses on the segments." She swiped to a second screen with an assortment of charts and graphs.

"So, it's anything to do with violence that's been targeted. It's some sort of threat," said a deep-voiced man with thick, drooping eyebrows. He sat back in his chair as though he had single-handedly solved the obvious.

"Well…upon superficial perusal of the contents and the data, it does seem that violence is the primary target. But…" Allegra switched to another screen. A new list of words appeared.

Punishment
Anger
Sin
Hellfire

"It appears there is a distinct epistemology behind the attacks. It's not just bloodshed by humans against humans, but also forms of harsh, metaphysical interaction."

"I'm afraid you're going to have to explain that for the uh…non-experts," Fielding chuckled, in the strange way, Ray thought, the less educated often have of belittling those more knowledgeable.

Allegra cast him another of her smiles. "Violence in the afterlife, forms of violence against humans by supernatural forces." Fielding looked blank. "What we might call 'God.'"

Fielding joined the bobbing heads of the committee, comprehension finally dawning upon them.

"So, if all references to violence have gone, what are they going to target next?" a white-haired woman in a purple and yellow suit asked from across the table, looking up from one of the papers. From his seat, Ray could not tell if her eyebrows were just very faint or whether she had shaved them off completely.

"Well, that's not quite what has happened. We need to go back to our definition of violence. If we understand this to be the infliction of bodily pain upon a person from one source or another, then yes, violence has disappeared from these three texts. However, it is my suspicion that the attack on violence, so to speak, is not over yet. Violence, as we are all very aware, comes in far more forms than just the physical."

The nods this time were portentous. More jaws tightened.

"If we broaden our definition to aggression, under which these verses still fall, I believe it is possible to identify a broader range of segments which are likely to be targeted."

Allegra swiped again to another screen split into three columns.

"As you'll see from the highlighted sections, it is certainly possible to define verses such as these as falling under the umbrella of aggression."

Your women are your fields, so go into your fields whichever way you like…

But I suffer not a woman to teach, nor to usurp authority over the man, but to be in silence…

When a parent sells a daughter as a slave, she shall not go free as other slaves do.

Eyes around the room were narrowed and strained, peering at the screen to read the verses that Allegra had presented in a tense and uncomfortable silence.

In 2040, in the aftermath of the war, global leaders seized the chance to amend the wrongs of previous millennia and passed a law that only those who identified as female could hold the highest positions of power. The male gender, they claimed, had been the perpetrators of global violence as far back as history recorded and had, thus, forfeited their hold on the reins of the world. The large disparity in the gender ratio by the turn of the decade, with women outnumbering men almost two to one, may have contributed to the swift passing of the bill, which also instituted a raft of equality laws ensuring equal pay and strict criminal punishment for gender-related crimes. This, of course, had done little to assuage the insecurities of many men who carried with them a sense of injustice in the face of their imposed equality. Nevertheless, the verses on the screen stood out as starkly alien, vestiges from a world unremembered. An unpalatable reminder of what humanity had once considered normal, even sacred.

"Aggression against former minorities." Allegra swiped again, revealing a list of references to verse numbers. "My current guess, based on the data, is that a broader definition of aggression will be the target of any future attacks."

"But why would anyone care about erasing references to types of violence that no longer exist?" asked the droopy-eyebrowed man.

Allegra tilted her head, examining his face. Her expression was direct and yet dissociated, as if she might be looking at the man and through him at the same time. "As I told my colleague here earlier…" She gestured to Ray. "…my job is the *what*. The *who* and the *how* are not my domain."

III

Somewhere below Ray's third-floor room in a building on the outer reaches of Freedom Point, an automatic door creaked open and closed. Open and closed. It sounded like an old rocking chair, a collection of grating, disparate notes. Ray knew he could easily log into the hotel's web portal with a swipe of his finger and file a maintenance report, but it was likely to go unnoticed until the morning anyway and the thought of getting out of bed and allowing gravity to strip him of any vestiges of sleep was more than he could bear.

Open. Close. Open. Close.

There were seconds, perhaps when the breeze plucked up the courage to push against it, that Ray thought the perpetual motion had stopped. Only for the sounds to start again.

When they had finally been allowed to leave the department, the sun had started to set. The city was lit with an eerie reddish glow, as though they had stepped into a developing room. Colors were distorted, shadows even shadier. Grays became blacks and blacks became empty voids.

The light that came in through the chink in the blackout blinds was the same color as the cold stone of the building he was staying in—a mix of the insomniac city glow and an unlocatable moon somewhere beyond the dome.

Ray's head was numb from the endless questions about cataloging he had been forced to answer in the meetings that followed their initial briefing. The numbness made sounds and sensations all the more sharp and everything else feel surreal. The maid who had greeted him in the hotel foyer, the once brightly colored furniture now a collection of dull and dusty shades from overuse and under-appreciation, had a mechanical fault somewhere in her internal wiring and one of her eyelids twitched incessantly. There was a slight scratch in the silicone just above her collarbone.

Open. Close. Open. Close.

Ray flung back the thin covers and swung his legs out of bed. His tablet was charging in the wall port by the window. At least, if he could not sleep, he could distract himself from the noise that seemed to have synchronized itself with his breathing.

As he passed the gap in the blinds, which had refused to shut no matter how many times he tried the controls, something caught his eye. In the corner of the scrappy garden that circled the building, he saw a thin plume of smoke. It twirled up gracefully, catching the light of the lamp that hung overhead. Following the trail down, Ray saw the back of a head of thick sleek hair that also seemed to glimmer in the nocturnal glow, clipped back neatly.

In the garden, transfixed by the stillness broken only by the willowy dance of the smoke, Ray paused.

"Do you mind if I join you?"

Allegra turned to him, unstartled. "Not at all. I was just…thinking."

Ray nodded. He sat down on the opposite end of the bench. The buildings, the same they had passed on their way into the city, rose up around them like giant tombstones, their stone interrupted by a braille-like pattern of illuminated windows. Every now and then, one would be extinguished, and somewhere else another would wake.

"I was thinking about questions." Allegra took a long drag on her vape and exhaled the smoke in a long, slow stream. Ray once again thought he could smell almonds. "Today, in the meeting, I said I was interested in the *what*. And this is true. I have been possessed, ever since I was first informed about these disappearances, with what was going missing."

Ray watched the smoke rise, twirling in the yellow light of the streetlamp as though inscribing her thoughts as she spoke them.

"But the *what* is bigger than that. It's not just what is disappearing. It's what are they disappearing from?"

Ray turned to look at her now. Her brow was furrowed, and she was staring straight ahead, her vape balanced between her fingers.

"Sacred texts."

"But isn't that strange?" Allegra turned her head toward Ray slightly.

"The whole thing is strange. Unsettling."

"Of course, texts disappearing is strange. But why sacred texts? Texts that are as far removed from us now as the Epic of Gilgamesh or the hieroglyphs on ancient Egyptian obelisks. If you wanted to make a statement, why not remove text from the constitution, from the bill of rights and freedoms, from the Magna Carta?"

"Too difficult to access?"

"Not at all. There are copies in every American and English history book. And these are still taught today."

"So, why sacred texts?"

"Why indeed?"

Ray turned back to the buildings before them, the vast structures thrown up in the aftermath of almost a decade of war to house those recruited to ensure that conflict never again plagued the scarred face of the earth. The buildings in which thousands went about their lives every day unaware of the creeping threat that was seeping through the systems designed to protect them. People whose lives were predicted and predictable down to their very heartbeats, whose own dreams could be deciphered by the data they uploaded second by second.

Somewhere in the distance, Ray could hear the door squeaking.

Open. Close. Open. Close.

"Where is this all coming from?" He looked up at Allegra, who had stood, blocking the insipid lamplight, casting him in a grateful shadow. It gave her hair a burnished copper tinge and caught the outline of her suit.

"Yet another question. *What, where, who, how*? And *why*?" She smiled. "Perhaps that's the point of all this. The questions."

~

It was not until the almond scent had completely disappeared, some immeasurable moments after Allegra had left, that Ray stirred on the bench. His muscles were stiff from the cold that had permeated his skin from its metal bars.

It was not a conscious decision to walk in the opposite direction to the hotel, but something inside him knew that the chink in the blinds, the lifeless colors of the worn furniture, and the unrelenting complaint of the door somewhere in the building that would greet him was more than he could bear.

The knowledge that the navigation system in his tablet and smartwatch would guide him home no matter how far he wandered gave him at least the freedom to walk without paying attention to road signs. But Ray was aware, at the back of his skull, of a gnawing craving for the feeling of being lost. He was never lost. Being lost was a historical concept. Even if one abandoned their gadgets, the chip implants—made mandatory in the aftermath of the war, upon which the entirety of one's personal data was stored and via which a person's temperature, blood pressure, hydration levels, stress levels, cholesterol levels, location, and surface contact with any technological device was perpetually collected and uploaded—all it took was access to one's personal account to immediately geolocate them to within a square meter. In theory, one had the right to be lost. But no one had the freedom to be so.

Like a heavy hand always on one's shoulder, somehow, it added to the weight. The weight the world seemed to carry. The weight no one spoke about but every advertisement, caustically cheerful, aimed to lighten; the vitamin B-enriched dairy substitutes, the daily doses of SSRI antidepressants and serotonin-boosting supplements, CBD-enhanced ready-meals, the banning of negative, scaremongering news items in the daily broadcasts, the chirpy affirmations from which it was impossible to unsubscribe that popped up on the smartwatch screens the moment one opened their eyes.

It was only in the aftermath of war that the world realized that peace did not equal happiness. The world had fought for peace, or had at least arrived at it, but in the process, they had forgotten something, lost it along the way. In truth, it had not been there before the war either, but at least war had brought with it a promise of its return. In the years leading up to the conflict, and even more so during it, people had lived out of fear. The fear that they would not live kept them determined to stay alive—the fear that they would die of hunger, of starvation, of radiation, of bombs, at gunpoint by the mobs that ran riot through the streets. As many did. Millions did. Billions. What was left of meaning by the eve of war was annihilated and buried in an unmarked grave somewhere on the outskirts of civilization when the peace treaties were signed.

Everyone had an explanation; population boom, climate change, food shortages, droughts, famine. They lived now in an era of explanation. But all meaning had been lost. Pulpits and podiums alike were silent. And those who had hung around until the last to listen left. Earth was a planet forsaken. Except that the conviction that there had been nothing to be abandoned by in the first place only served to intensify the universal sense of alienation.

Ray walked through the gate at the edge of the garden and turned down a dark lane between two buildings, indistinguishable from the others in shape, size, and looming sense of presence. A row of twenty-four-hour shop fronts, identical but for the signs over their entrances, were illuminated, their automated payment systems that placed charges directly to a person's account as they walked out of the door with their goods alleviating the need for any customer service staff. A few weary businessmen and women in rumpled suits meandered in and out of the doors. Ray stopped outside one of them.

"Freedom Fried Chicken*!" clucked its garish red and yellow sign, two intersecting drumsticks in a circle hung from an outstretched pole at a right angle to the window. Two women inside were queuing at a kiosk that periodically spat out orders from an automated kitchen system somewhere beyond the back wall. A small sign in the corner of the window caught Ray's eye.

All chicken meat is lab-grown. No animals were harmed in the manufacturing of Freedom Fried Chicken products.

The smashing of a bottle cut through the city's nocturnal hum. Somewhere down the road ahead of him between the pools of two streetlamps, a woman was stumbling, trying to figure out where the bottle she had been carrying had gone.

Ray peered into the yellow gloom. She seemed to be crying. He started toward her, a sudden surge of energy dispelling his lethargy.

"Do you need help, miss?" he called into the sepia shadows.

"She's fine, sir. Thank you for your concern."

Out of a large transport pod that had pulled up suddenly beside her, a man and a woman in dark uniforms had appeared. They scooped an arm under each of the woman's and maneuvered her jerkily into the pod.

"Is she okay?" Ray was closer now, though the insides of the pod were still obscured by the darkness.

Having bundled the woman now strategically inside and sliding the doors closed, the man approached Ray, emerging large from the shadows. "Everything is fine, sir. I'd advise you to be on your way."

It was possible to end one's life. One certainly had the right to. But the freedom to do so was also debatable. In an era in which life on earth was dwindling, to contribute in any way to one's own premature demise had become taboo. Survivor's guilt had been replaced by survivor's burden. The burden of life. Life on a planet that humanity had all but destroyed. Knowingly. Life on a planet that was unlikely to recover fully, no matter how much the news broadcasts celebrated the opposite. To bring life into such a planet, still raw from the memories of the cruel depths of human capacity, was widely seen as selfish, no matter how much government advertisements encouraged, practically bribed women to give birth. Only those who had forgotten quickly the terrible potential of humankind took to their beds to procreate, and that in and of itself was seen as a tragedy.

Life was entirely predictable. It held no meaning, no surprises, and the promise only of death. Philosophers deliberated. The point of life was life, they concluded. A tautology that drove even the sanest silently mad.

When dawn broke, the air across the city staining a spectrum of fleshy tones, Ray found himself standing at the edge of the vast, immaculate lawn surrounding the parliament building.

The streets were quiet. A slumber seemed to have overtaken even the inanimate. A travel pod trundled past quietly, sweeping the edges of the sidewalks with a soft shushing sound. Ray bent down and pulled off his shoes, and then his bright blue socks, baggy around the ankles now, and stepped onto the grass. He felt individual blades crumpling underfoot. It was cold against his skin. Prickly.

The lawn banked at a slight slope. He walked toward the enormous stone lettering, at this distance no longer symbols, nothing more than curves and lines of smooth sandstone. Ray stepped onto the cool stone, registering the dustiness of its surface. His footsteps whispered as he walked toward the grass at the other side. Slowly, he turned, taking in the panorama of rock that encircled him at his feet. Tiredness had left him, though exhaustion had taken root. Ray sat down gently, his back toward the parliament building, facing the downward slope, and the mass of steel and concrete beyond.

~

He bought a can of *InstaShave* and a new tube of his usual brand of SPF lotion from one of the convenience stores he had passed, and a clean shirt and socks from a gentleman's clothing outlet further down the street. He locked the door of the bathroom off the foyer of the Prognostication building, slipping past the pink-haired receptionist who was bent over a drawer of digital name tags that was refusing to close. Ray's reflection, lathered in the thick pink foam covering his jaw, looked gray. He pulled at the dark spaces beneath his eyes and covered them in the tinted SPF.

Ray did not see Allegra except for a brief moment in the cafeteria when they exchanged waves from the opposite sides of the room; her leaving, him arriving.

The meetings—briefings, consultations, system deliberations—seemed to stretch on for even longer than the day before. By the time five o'clock arrived, Ray could barely summon the energy to walk to the transport stop. He swiped his finger over the sensor beside his hotel room door and fell heavily onto his bed.

It was dark when he awoke, and though he had been sure it must be well past midnight, he was surprised to see it was only a little after eight.

A message flashed onto his tablet screen. An invitation. Ray, still woozy from sleep, tapped the notification, which sprang open. It was from a Richard Greene. Ray wracked his memory for a Richard Greene.

Heard you were in town.
Fancy meeting up for a drink and reminisce about
college days?

A face swam groggily into view. A dorm. A fellow freshman. Citizenship classes. There was a location link and a reservation.

Ray had lost touch with all his college friends soon after graduating and assumed the war had claimed most of them. He knew had he opened the Suggested Acquaintances in the Area app that it would undoubtedly have told him of Richard Greene's continued existence. But it had not occurred to Ray that he might know someone who worked in Freedom Point.

He sat on the edge of the bed contemplating his options. No doubt Richard Greene would have seen him open his message, so it was too late to pretend he had never received it. He weighed the guilt of the man's disappointment against his own desire to avoid unnecessary human contact.

Sleep had now evaded him, swaying his decision. He folded his clothes neatly, placing them into the laundry compartment of his suitcase, and stepped into the shower.

Had Ray been asked to pick Richard Greene out of a lineup, he would have struggled. Time and lifestyle had smudged and widened the man's features, and thinned his hair, despite, Ray was sure, the use of products to counter both.

Richard slapped Ray heartily on the back, a gesture Ray concluded must be a routine feature of human interaction in the city. He was a small, broad man. Good-natured, from what Ray remembered, but otherwise run of the mill. The type that made his way through life on the basis of his social skills rather than any actual talent. His hair was braided closely against his head, intertwined with yellow and blue threads, tied together at the back of his head.

They sat at the raised, round, glass tabletop, perched on faux-leather stools, and swiped their fingers, summoning the drinks menu and digital drinks counters.

"And you're working at the Lit Hub, I saw? Still in Zone 4?"

Ray nodded to the barman who had set down their drinks, topped with a coaster upon which was balanced a small wrapper.

"That's right, never really left." Ray pulled open the wrapper and popped the blue pill under his tongue.

"These things are life savers." Richard chuckled. "Literally. Why didn't they have these when we were in college? Would have saved my liver, and probably my grades too!" He took a swig of the frothy beer from the tall, thin glass. "Probably relationships as well, if I'm honest."

"You're partnered?" Ray put his beer down on his coaster. "Me? No." Richard shook his head. "Soledad and I, we tried, you know, but the war brought out the worst in people. And, you know, we…went our separate ways." He shrugged and then tipped back the glass again, emptying it. The bar on his drinks counter crept up toward his maximum recommended blood alcohol level.

"And who needs a partner when you can have a companion, eh?" He wiggled his eyebrows.

"Mmm." Ray took another sip of his beer.

"How about those new models? You have them where you are? The XVPs?"

Ray shook his head. "They seem much more advanced here." A flush of awkwardness at the implications of this statement surged up toward his cheeks, but Richard seemed oblivious.

"You know what's weird, though? Cheers." He watched the barman set down his second drink. Ray noticed the faint glow beneath the barman's watch as he placed the glass on the coaster. "They always insist on sending me tall ones. Weirdly tall. Six-foot, shoe sizes bigger than mine, and hands the size of my face." He raised his open palm and placed it over his face as though donning a mask. "They still won't let you design your own. I figure that'll be the next big thing. It'll be expensive. Although, I can't think why it's cheaper for them to model them based on your preferences." He shrugged again.

Though the conversation was somewhat uncomfortable, Ray had at least been glad that Richard was happily bearing the brunt of it. The man's gabble about companions, apartment prices in Freedom Point, his job, and the latest model of smartwatch, which he unclipped and dangled proudly in the air, alleviated the need for Ray to make any real personal contribution.

By the time Ray had finished his second glass, Richard was on his fifth. He had overridden the flashing warning that he was about to exceed his recommended limit and ordered another. He scanned the bar blearily, his eyes glassy. Conversation slowed. The late-night humdrum of chatter ebbed and flowed around them, filling the silence that hovered over their table.

"You know, I've got six years, Ray. Six years left." He tapped the watch on his wrist with a leaden finger. "They say I could retire. Move back to wherever, Connecticut. Retire. They're not allowed to fire me. Discrimination laws and all that. And what would I do? Sit on my porch and look out over solar fields?" He laughed through his nose, his mouth unmoving. "How long you got?"

"Uh…twenty…twenty-something. Thereabouts." Ray swallowed.

"What are you going to do?"

"What am I going to do?"

"Yeah. For the rest of your life."

The question had never occurred to him. How would he fill the time that stretched before him? Work. Eat. Sleep. Work. Sleep. Retire at some point. Characterless milestones on a journey that could be anyone's. And then what? Ray looked at the man sitting before him, each blink a second slipping away. He wondered when he would start counting.

"You know, I used to think… Maybe if I was a good person, I'd get a good life, you know? I suppose I did get a good life, in some senses. I survived, didn't I? Maybe I should have been better? But they tell you it doesn't even work like that. Morality, and all that jazz." Richard waved a hand unsteadily in the air. "Good citizenship, that's what they call it now. It's just all fucking word games though, isn't it?"

Ray looked discreetly around the room, a panic rising in his throat. No one seemed to be paying them any attention.

"I could leave now, and it wouldn't make any difference. Just a blip in some graph somewhere. They'd identify a replacement in a couple of hours, I'm sure. Fill my apartment before I'm cremated. You know they have a state-sponsored spreading service now. For ashes. In case you've got no one to do it for you. They get one of these...flesh molds." He waved his hand in the direction of the bartender. "Send 'em out to do it. There's a list of places you can pick from, as a reward for contributing to energy production by choosing to go up in smoke rather than take up habitable space. Want to know where I picked?" He raised his eyebrows in a question, dragging his gaze up to Ray's face. Ray looked at his forehead.

"The Grand Canyon. The Grand fucking Canyon." This time he laughed aloud, though his eyes still showed no hint of a smile. "I didn't know where any of the other places were." He reached for his tablet, teetering precariously on the stool. "Here," he said, unrolling it. "I'll read you the list, and you can pick."

A wild desperation welled in Ray's chest. "There's nothing you want to do before you leave? Places you want to see? Memories you want to make?"

Richard lowered the tablet to the table, the crematorium app mercifully still unopened.

"What's the point? It'll all be gone with me."

"Sense of fulfillment, distraction? Leaving a mark, maybe?"

"What, like charity? Anything you leave behind gets redistributed. And the welfare funds, you know, no one needs charity in this day and age."

"What about kids? Someone to remember you."

"I got six years left, Ray. Six years. By the time I find an egg donor and a surrogate, I'll have maximum five years with the kid. And then what, leave them an orphan? In this fucking hell hole, where they'll never see the sun? Living like we do, at best under a fucking dome. At worst, burrowed away like fucking...I don't know... moles. Worms. Building, building, building, for what?

So we can fucking destroy it all again? What the fuck's the point?"

The condensation from Ray's drink had pooled on the coaster in a wet ring. He lifted the glass and tipped back the remainder of the contents. Richard was fiddling with the controls on his smartwatch. "Bastard thing, I still can't figure out how to stop it from reminding me to sleep."

It wasn't until the pod that Ray had helped Richard clamber into had rounded the corner of the block that Ray checked his smartwatch: 2.35 a.m.

The time blinked up at him before being replaced by a scrolling torrent of notifications.

"Fuck." Ray tapped the screen anxiously, forgetting he had left it on silent while he slept. He scrolled through them rapidly, feeling his pulse quickening in his neck.

He looked around wildly, trying to get his bearings. His brain was still sluggish. *App*, he remembered, *transport app*. There was a transport pod a minute and a half away.

"Where would you like to go today, Ray?" it asked him cheerfully.

"Prognostics Department," he said, holding the button for the microphone.

~

"Where the fuck have you been?" said Fielding's brief expression from across the room. The meeting room was filled with committee members, surprisingly alert, who largely ignored Ray as he crept in through the door.

The ascent to the 356th floor had made Ray feel queasy, and Fielding's silent reprimand did little to abate the effusion of saliva under his tongue.

He slid into his seat next to Allegra. Her hands were folded on top of a small pile of books. She was facing

Fielding, her hair hung loosely down the back of her shirt, a deep forest green.

"For the benefit of those who have just joined us," Fielding was saying, "there has been a new wave of attacks." Ray felt the tepid sweat that covered his back turn cold. "Doc, you've taken a provisional look at what's been removed. Want to fill us in?"

Allegra stood to her feet. She lay the books out side by side on the desktop in front of her, flipping each one open to a specific spot, the pages sliding against each other, sounding like the slicing of a blade.

She looked up slowly from the books to an indeterminate point somewhere behind the audience before her. The screen came to life on the wall.

"As you'll see from the pages, the same texts were targeted again. Primary texts. Some twenty percent of the remaining contents have been erased. With the help of a colleague at the Lit Hub here, I managed to obtain print copies of the texts." She swept her hand over the open books. "And, while I have not had much time to analyze the new data, there does appear to be a theme."

"Violence?" asked a voice from somewhere in the room. "Aggression?" another committee member chimed. "Women." Allegra's voice was level, cool, almost as though she might be reading a weather forecast, not the results of the most recent attack of cultural terrorism.

"Women?" Confused glances were exchanged around the room. Mutterings arose. "What do you mean 'women'?"

"There hasn't been time to copy them out, but if you'll remember the examples of verses I showed you when we first met… I would show them to you on the screen again except, of course, they've disappeared." A faint smile crossed Allegra's lips.

"Slaves and fields, or something?" a woman to her left asked, shaking her head as if to dislodge the memory.

"Something along those lines, yes." Allegra nodded slowly. "I'll read them to you again." She placed her finger halfway down the page of the first book before her:

"Your women are your fields, so go into your fields whichever way you like…" She slid her finger over to the second, clearing her throat. "But I suffer not a woman to teach, nor to usurp authority over the man, but to be in silence…"

"Silence, that was it." The woman to her left grimaced. "When a parent sells a daughter as a slave, she shall not go free as other slaves do." Allegra looked back up from the pages, her expression unreadable.

"So, you were right. It's aggression, like you said." The man with the dropping eyebrows, nodding, sliced his finger through the air as though he might somehow also lay claim to her earlier prediction.

"I'm afraid not. Not entirely." Allegra slid her hands into the pockets of her trousers, a rich brown shade. "You see, I predicted that any new attack would target instances of aggression against former minorities. Provisional examinations reveal, however, that this wave seems to have been far more extensive than mere aggression." She took a hand out of her pocket and placed it on one of the books. "This time, all references to distinct genders or any other classifications of humans have been entirely removed."

"What do you mean?" Ray asked, surprised at the sound of his own voice.

"I mean any use of gendered pronouns or signifiers, any verses addressing or concerning women specifically, as well as those addressing particular nations or populations, are no longer present in these texts. I've not had much time to look, and this needs further analysis, but so far, this is what stands out as obvious."

"The word 'woman' does not exist in those pages?" Fielding nodded his head toward the texts.

"It does not."

"What about men?" the man with the droopy eyebrows asked.

"'Man' is a gendered signifier." Allegra flipped a couple of pages, as though to double-check.

"So, they're gone too." Ray watched the thin pages float down as she flipped them.

Allegra exhaled deeply. "Yes, they're gone too."

The rest of the meeting, commandeered by Fielding, consisted of a revised strategy to encrypt the scanned documents and to ramp up the transferal process of all sacred literature to the Freedom network.

At five past five, Ray slid the door of the transport pod closed behind them with a metallic thud. Allegra was twirling the point of her jade clasp between her thumb and forefinger, her brow furrowed. They climbed the hotel steps in silence.

At the door of the elevator, Allegra turned to make her way to her room.

"I don't suppose," Ray began. Allegra stopped, turning her head back toward him. His words hung in the dimly lit hall. "I don't suppose you're any closer to an answer?"

She gave him a tired smile; honest, genuine, but weary. "Only more questions." He nodded his head. "Good night, Ray."

V

By 2049, the populace, or what was left of it, was as surprised that they had once lived with overt sexual discrimination as they were that they had once built economies on the basis of racial slavery. The rampant abuse of young women in the film industry, the polishing of glass ceilings, and the unequal burdens of parenthood were explained with the same logic as female genital mutilation, forced marriages, and honor killings. These were remnants of a time in which there had once been contextual causes that had gone unchecked until the world woke up to find the dynamics of society so drastically changed that not only could it no longer be tolerated, but it was also possible to put a final stop to it.

Just as philosophers conveniently forgot, ignored, or explained away with "context" Aristotle's deeply misogynistic views toward women, just as landmark institutions of knowledge and progress forgot, ignored, or explained away their vast sums of money from stolen lands and stolen lives, so too did religious authorities interact with their uncomfortable histories. The opiate of the masses had become one of the very things the masses numbed themselves against.

By the turn of the fifth decade of the third millennium, the attempts at explanations had ceased. Religious groups, where they still existed, were treated with the same amused pity and arm's length tolerance with which traveling circus acts had once been greeted; their practices curious, vaguely interesting, but unwelcome for long periods.

It had been the subject of much debate, during the Book Drive, whether it might not be wiser simply to ban literature that espoused practices contrary to the laws and principles that governed the post-war world.

A consensus was eventually reached that such a move itself would be inconsistent with the principles they had chosen to live by: freedom and liberty.

And besides, history spoke volumes to the fact that attempts to ban anything always resulted in underground streams of such behavior, from ideas to alcohol. They would far rather know what people were reading and take action accordingly.

The vast tomes of legislation regarding incitement to violence, hate, prejudice, and discrimination, plus the mandatory registering of all sermon and religious ceremony contents, delivered the desired effect: peace and predictions.

~

Ray did not see Allegra in the cafeteria, nor in Fielding's briefing—brasher and barkier than ever. He spent the day escorted from system room to system room. The myriad of shades of sage and olive green that adorned the walls of the cold rooms, supposedly promoting an atmosphere of strength and sophistication, left Ray with a foreboding sense of nausea and an ache behind one eye. The drone of category labels, inclusion, and exclusion criteria, and interminable clicking, had left little room for him to think of anything other than a stream of digital files, migrating like wildebeest from one arid grassland to another.

It was the sight of Allegra's face, composed and concentrating, on the department steps, the late afternoon light giving her hair a metallic sheen, that brought him back to an awareness of the strangeness he was surrounded by. He cleared his throat.

"Long day?" she asked him amiably.

Ray smiled, for the first time that day, he realized.

"You must be hungry," she said, turning to walk down the steps. "When was the last time you had sushi?"

"Good sushi?" he asked, thinking hard, trying to recall.

"If it came in a packet it doesn't count." She turned, having reached the bottom of the stairs. Her brows were clenched sternly, but a grin played around the corners of her mouth.

"In that case, never."

"Good." She unknitted her brows. "Then follow me."

"How did you find this place?" Ray asked, relieved that they had finally arrived and he could take the load off his feet. The last time he had walked so far was when the communications system had gone down in the early days of the Lit Hub and he'd been forced to walk from the basement up to Monica's office on the third floor.

The shop front looked like any other, but inside, softly lit by lotus-shaped lanterns, the restaurant looked unlike anything Ray had ever seen. The walls were covered in thick bamboo stems, and in the center of the room was a small pool with a trickling water feature, the quiet gurgling constituting the only background noise to the low chatter of a spattering of customers.

"I asked a friend," she said, following the waiter to a table in the corner.

Allegra slid the pink orchid in the small glass vase to the edge of the table by the neat pile of chopsticks and crisp napkins. She clasped her hands on the table in front of her. Ray concentrated on the napkins, feeling the fabric between his fingers. They seemed to be cotton.

"It's all natural." Allegra was watching him. "The chopsticks are bamboo. And the fish are all real." Ray glanced toward the pond. "Those too," she laughed.

"Oh, you meant the…" Ray nodded. "Of course… Is there a menu?"

"No menu. The chef simply cooks whatever is fresh and available."

Ray looked up at her surprised.

"Don't worry, I trust her." Allegra's smile was wide. "I suddenly had a craving for something…untampered with. I know we're supposedly very lucky to have all these substitutes, but I can't help wondering what it is that I'm eating."

"Maybe that's why the pond is here. As a reminder." Allegra laughed. "Perhaps."

The sushi arrived on a large bamboo board, in the shape of a swimming koi. Allegra reached for a set of chopsticks. She held them deftly between her knuckles.

"Don't overthink it," she said, demonstrating to Ray how to clasp the sushi between them and dip it in the flat bowls of sauce.

Ray chose a piece carefully. The dark, mottled seaweed exterior popped as his teeth sank into it. The rice, smooth, sticky, and rich, had a delicate, almost creamy flavor, and the fish inside was tender, ever so slightly oily, with a powerful, salty kick that sent saliva washing around his mouth.

"Good?" asked Allegra, reading the response from the intensity of his facial expressions. "Try this one—it's my favorite." She pointed with the tip of her chopsticks to a thinner piece, with the rice encasing a collection of vegetables and fish that Ray could not identify. It was coated in a pea-green powder. Ray crunched down on the vegetables, tasting cucumber and crab. His eyes widened: a sudden surge of cold heat rushed up his nasal passages. He coughed, trying to alleviate the sensation that every inhale of air was both fiery and frozen.

"Wasabi powder," Allegra laughed, pouring him a glass of water. "Sorry, I should have warned you. It'll pass, I promise." She gave him a conciliatory look.

Ray took a long gulp. Now that the initial burning had subsided, the tingling aftermath was rather pleasant.

"What's the pink stuff?" He peered at a small porcelain bowl, inside which lay thin slivers of something a pale, translucent pink.

"That," she said, picking up a piece delicately, allowing a drop of juice to fall back into the bowl before she placed it on top of a piece of sushi, "is pickled ginger."

"Ginger? I thought ginger was yellow."

"There's a chemical in the new roots that reacts with the vinegar, turning it pink. Try a bit on its own first."

With the focus of a surgeon, Ray pinched a thin piece between his chopsticks and extracted it from the bowl.

"Oh," he said, surprised. It was tangy, warm as he expected it would be, but also sweet, fragrant, and crunchy. He picked up another. "Now this, I can eat," he laughed.

They ate slowly, with a quiet, comfortable relish, savoring the array of flavors and textures—the stickiness, crunchiness, saltiness, the unexpected aromas, the occasional bite of spice—and the sense of having smuggled something natural, an experience that defied the net of the "normal" in Freedom Point.

In response to a few words from Allegra that Ray did not quite catch, the waiter brought over a small tray. Gracefully, he set down two small ceramic cups, and a bulbous jug, with a thin neck and blossoming lip. Next to them he placed a bowl of what looked like bright green, slightly furry, seed pods.

"Edamame," the waiter told them.

Ray glanced at the man's wrists, expecting to catch a glimpse of the dull internal light that belied his humanness. He was surprised instead to see branches of thin blue and purple veins, and a rippling tendon. The waiter smiled at him. Ray smiled back.

With a musical trickle, Allegra poured out a clear liquid into the two small cups. With a nod, she picked up the vessel, cupping it in the palm of her hand. Guiding it with the fingers of her other, she raised it to her lips, taking a sip.

Ray copied her. It tasted clean, only very slightly sweet, a fermented bite warming his throat.

Allegra set her cup down on the table. She seemed to be staring at the koi pond, though her gaze was not focused. Ray noticed she had a small, shiny scar just above her right eyebrow.

She exhaled deeply, turning to face him, though her eyes remained on the water.

"Did you know, the world's largest cave was once in Vietnam? It was called the Hang Sơn Đoòng." She pronounced the name with long, slow syllables. "It doesn't exist anymore, but I visited it once. It was so big it had its own ecosystem, a subterranean rainforest." Her fingers were still on the rim of her cup. "It was formed by a rushing underground river. Imagine the force of it. Carving, over generations, flowing, pushing, incessant. Determined. You walk into the cave, and you see the walls, these alien formations of stalactites, the dense mossy surfaces, the pools, and you forget that it was the river that did this. All on its own. Quietly, unnoticeably, it created this space."

She blinked, bringing her gaze back to Ray, catching him in a moment of unexpected eye contact. He noticed again how dark her irises were before he lowered his eyes to his cup.

"I don't think this is a terrorist attack." Her words took Ray by surprise.

"You don't?" he asked her.

"No." She shook her head, a strand of hair falling loose from behind her ear. She leaned down to her bag and pulled out a book. Ray's eyes darted around the room, flitting from face to face, but the remaining handful of customers were concentrating on their food or deep in conversation.

She slid her finger between the pages, interrupted by the tongues of brightly colored markers. She lay the book flat at a right angle to the both of them, and stroked her palms across the pages as though to smooth them. She had highlighted various sections in a pale yellow marker.

"See here?" She pointed to a verse. "And here." She slid her finger to another highlighted section farther down the page. "It's the same throughout each of the texts. I didn't notice it before. I suppose I was too caught up in this idea of violence."

Ray read the verses again. "But these have nothing to do with violence."

"Precisely," she said, flipping to another page and pointing out another section.

"Or women." Ray peered closer at the verse. "They're about…"

"They're about God." She turned the book toward her and read the verse aloud. "'Do not cling to me, for I have not yet ascended to the Father; but go to my brothers and say to them, "I am ascending to my Father and your Father, to my God and your God."' This is Jesus speaking to Mary Magdalen."

"So, references to God as Father have disappeared?" Ray looked at her quizzically.

"Far more than that." She lay another book from her bag on the table. "References to God as 'He.'"

Ray laughed. "But surely that's all references." He had opened the book in front of him, reading the cover, The Quran. He was flipping through the pages, reading all the sections highlighted in yellow.

"Not quite." Allegra placed her finger on the page Ray had reached. "In some places, God is referred to in the plural."

Ray followed her finger to the word. This time, he read the verse aloud: "We have, without doubt, sent down the Message; and We will assuredly guard it." He paused. "But what does it mean?"

"That, I'm still not sure of. The 'what' still seems to be unfolding. But if there's one thing we can be sure of, it changes the 'who.' The terrorism theory made sense in the light of the verses on violence. But this..." She gestured with an open palm to the books in front of her. "This is no terrorist message."

Questions, of various sorts and shades, battered the insides of Ray's skull. What, why, who, how? No matter which way he phrased it, he knew he would be met with the same response—there were no answers yet. Only more questions.

Perhaps it was the warm glow of the sake behind his cheeks, perhaps it was the reddish glow of the sunset, perhaps it was the intensity of the curiosity that had, for now, shunted out the fear he had carried around in the pit of his stomach, that made Ray decline the suggestion of a transport pod, and choose instead to walk the way back to the hotel. Allegra seemed pleased.

In company, the buildings did not seem quite so monstrous, and Ray noticed the vertical gardens that had been planted in many of the walls along the streets they chose. They were on the other side of the city to their hotel, meaning they needed to cross Parliament Square. In the distance, down the long road that led to the parliament building, Ray could see the needle glinting in the setting sunlight.

The roads seemed strangely quiet for this time of the evening. Streets usually bustled before dark with eager customers scooping up goods on their way home from the office, or strolling toward the virtual reality cinemas that were dotted around the city.

It was not until they were a block away from the city's center that the sound of a low, rhythmic thudding became apparent.

Ray looked at Allegra, who had heard it too. She raised her eyebrows, apparently as unaware of its source as he was. Abruptly, the drumming came to a stop, and the sounds of a voice over a microphone, tinny at this distance and sharp, ricocheted off the sides of the buildings. Trumpets sounded. The voice returned; the words discernable now that they had moved closer:

"…And on this day, under the protection of the dome, we renew our oath, our pledge, to rid ourselves from the dark shadow of war for eternity."

The loud ripple of a cheer followed.

Ray and Allegra rounded the corner. Enormous screens had been erected around the square, projecting a face in three-dimensional definition. Among the screens, stretching out from a huge pyramidal stage that had been rigged in front of the stone lettering, a crowd writhed.

"We emerged from an age of ignorance. It is our duty to uphold the mantle of knowledge…" The words rang, bell-like, shuddering off the steel and stone surfaces. "To honor the art and science of full disclosure that we might never again stumble into the abyss of blindness, of certain oblivion."

The woman on the screen was scarlet-lipped, her face enlarged to the breadth of an apartment. Simultaneously, her words echoed from every corner of the square. Her bottom lip moved deliberately as she spoke, revealing thin, tightly packed teeth, white and resolute. Her eyes moved slowly, scanning the crowd.

"Let us stand," boomed her voice, "for our national, global anthem."

An even deeper hush fell over the square. The large white flag, the symbol of Freedom Point—the clean, uncomplicated color of peace—flapped gently above them.

The camera cut to the face of a child, her dark hair braided with white ribbons, and a set of rainbow beads about her small neck. She sang crisply, earnestly, filling the song with an emotion far too old and ancient for her age. *Unity, wisdom, certitude.* Eternal intangibles upon which their new world was built, just as old worlds had also been.

The child's final note quivered in the air. She looked up to the adults around her and the camera swung back to the face of the president, calm and commanding.

"And now," she said, slicing through the silence, "as we stand here after the sun has set on the ninth year of liberation and peace, it is my pleasure, as the first president of Freedom Point, to declare celebrations open!"

The camera panned out wide, revealing the woman in the white suit, who swung a velvet-tipped mallet in her red gloved hands hard against an enormous bronze gong. The twang, deep and fluidic, was drowned in a riot of clamorous applause, cheers, whistles, instruments, the crash of cymbals and drums as the band, poised behind the president, burst into a deafening strain of music and song. Lights, wired up to every possible surface, spurted out multicolored beams that swept through the vast polychromed congregation.

The music pounded; Ray's internal organs reverberated with the pulses of the bass that surged suddenly through the microphones. The crowd swelled, surrounding them like a wave. He felt something clasp his hand, and turned to see Allegra, who proceeded to pull him through the crashing tides of bodies. Limbs swayed about him; fingers, shoulders, faces, backs, and breasts brushed against him. The air seemed to be receding; he gulped for it, taking in only breaths of human scents—sweet, sour, warm, and fetid.

He concentrated on Allegra, her back, her outstretched arm, the hand to which he clung, the hair, which was periodically caught in the swooping beams and illuminated deep shades of colors unnamed.

They were nearing the edge of the lawn, swarmed with people. He knew that Allegra was trying to use it as a reference, to guide them through the crowds and to the other side from where they could reach their hotel. But the throngs thickened the closer they came to the center. He felt her fingers slide away from his as the bodies ebbed forward. He searched frantically for a glimpse of her but saw only the looming faces of people he had never met, awash with strange colors.

At first, he had thought it was the lights that cast people in these strange hues, but now that he had stopped, he noticed that their faces were painted, a throbbing kaleidoscope of smeared skin.

A woman rounded on him, her hair caked in green, and her face a mixture of orange and yellow. She placed her hands on his shoulders. She was mouthing something, her lips rounding, stretching, smiling. At first, Ray thought she must be talking to him, but then he realized that the reason he could not make out her words was because they were coming from all directions, from the mass of bodies surrounding him. They were all singing, chanting:

Freedoooommmmmm, freedoooommmmmm.

The vowels were long, the syllables hummed. It was the chorus to the song. The band picked up the pace, the tempo increasing, the words singular.

The woman ran her hands across Ray's cheeks, down his forearms. She took his hands and dragged them in the same motion across her skin. It was as she reached them past her collarbone, toward her pointed breasts, that Ray realized that what he had taken for clothes, a deep amethyst, were in fact nothing more than paint. Everybody was painted.

He pulled his hands from hers, recoiling, but the crowd pulsed, forcing them together. He felt her soft flesh compress against his chest and smelled the sharpness of the paint in her hair. His head swam. He wheeled around, only to find himself chest to chest with a man, eyes wild, who tipped his head back in what seemed a howl, beads around his neck swaying and glinting in the swiping beams of light.

Ray turned sideways and shouldered his way vehemently past. Hands clutched at him, snagging at his jacket, his belt, digging into spaces between his arms and legs. A heat seemed to rise around him, a dense torridity that bubbled and frothed. Ray clawed his way through the wall of flesh around him.

By the time he had reached the opposite shore of the crowd, he was gasping for breath. He leaned, his arm on the building, his lungs heaving, his back to the masses. Breakaway groups skittered and screamed down the sideroads, their hysteric peals rebounding around him. He saw one woman drag another by the arm into a doorway. They squirmed; their limbs entangled.

"You need a trip, man?"

Ray swung around. The man in front of him was holding out a handful of plastic-wrapped pills. Ray looked from the pills back to the man's face, daubed in silver, with blue rings around his red-tinged eyes. The hair on his chest was plastered against his skin in a thick, waxy aquamarine.

"He doesn't need anything," a voice sounded sharply. The man swung around to see Allegra behind him. He shrugged and lumbered off down the street. They watched him disappear in silence.

Allegra's face was streaked with color, her clothes too. She was no longer wearing shoes, and her black tights were ripped and laddered.

Ray looked down at his own garments, his jacket torn and smeared with sticky paint, his shoes scuffed, his cravat unraveled and dangling around his neck. The booms, muffled somewhat by the buildings, still resounded achingly in his skull.

"Come on." Allegra held out her hand. Ray took it gratefully.

They walked through the empty, illuminated streets, afraid that if they stopped, they might never start again. The structures had reclaimed their monstrosity, windows aflame with lights from within. The air was heavy, thick, still rippling even at this distance with the waves of sound that pulsed from the center of the city.

Ray looked up as they walked. The sky was black, and though there were no clouds beyond the dome, he could not see a single star. He felt suddenly suffocated, as though sure the events of the night, the writhing and gyrating of the crowds, had certainly sucked up all the oxygen beneath the dome. He felt Allegra squeeze his hand, and together they walked on.

After what seemed a lifetime, their hotel building emerged into view. Staggering up the steps and into the lift, Allegra keyed in the floor number. In the smudgey mirrored wall, Ray caught a glimpse of their reflections; mottled, stained. They stood close, listening to the faint chimes as the numbers ascended, their hands still clasped.

Perhaps it was the intensity of his exhaustion, or perhaps it was the fact that she did not loosen her grasp, that led Ray to follow Allegra down the long corridor to her hotel room without thought or question.

He slipped off his shoes at the door, stepping into the carpeted quiet, the walls a dusty pink. The awkwardness he might have otherwise expected—the taut sinews, the shallow breaths—was markedly absent, worn away not just by the ordeal of the evening, but the surrealness of the week.

Without speaking, Allegra handed him a robe from the back of the door, and he stepped into the bathroom, closing the door with a click. The shower stream came hot and fast against his skin. He watched the pale streaks of color weave their way over his legs and swirl down the drain.

The tiles were cold against his bare feet, and the robe, a deep inky blue, towel-like against his skin. He bundled his clothes into a ball and shoved them deep into the bin. He stared into the mirror. Scenes from the evening contorted themselves before him, colors and shapes seeping into his vision. He ran a comb from the shelf above the sink through his hair and stepped out into the bedroom.

In the quiet of the room, punctuated only by the hiss now of Allegra's shower, and the splashing of water against glass and tiles, Ray sat on the edge of the bed, his feet pressed into the carpet. The dressing table next to him was littered with bottles, creams, and a hairbrush with a jade handle.

He picked up a large tube of SPF, the same brand he had always used. He squeezed out a thin line of lotion onto his palm and rubbed his hands together. He ran them across his face—his forehead and across his chin. He stared absently at his reflection, only vaguely familiar, like a memory of the face of a loved one long after they had departed.

Allegra emerged from the bathroom, her feet padding across the carpet. Her robe was tied around her waist and she had rolled the sleeves away from her slender wrists. Her hair, scraped back away from her face, looked almost black now that it was wet.

She walked to the side of the bed and gently pulled back the covers. Ray stood, watching her. She pulled the blanket up over her, leaving the other half of the bed still exposed, her arm outstretched.

Slowly, he climbed in next to her, laying his head gently on her arm. He turned to face her. Her eyes closed. He could smell almonds.

The lights, sensing the absence of movement in the room, dimmed into darkness. Ray felt Allegra's fingers intertwine with his own, pulling them gently to settle over the knot on her robe. Though he could not hear her breathing, he could feel it, just as he felt the warmth of her emanating through the fabric, the cold of her fingers against his. He closed his eyes.

"I made love to my husband the night before he was killed. He was the last human being I slept with." Allegra's voice was low, though she did not whisper. "That was twelve years ago. He was a teacher at a high school before the war. He was killed by a stray bullet to the neck on his way home from his mother's house. I often wonder how long it took for him to die."

She sighed, her chest rising and falling heavily. "For a year afterwards, I felt like I had something lodged in my throat. I couldn't shift it. And then one day, I woke up, and it had gone. But I knew I'd never make love to another man again."

Ray listened. She continued, her voice low but crisp:

"No matter how realistic they make companions, it's comforting to know they will always be too perfect. Whoever designs them forgot that humans are messy, flawed, and selfish. Robots can't be selfish. So, it will never feel the same as making love to a human."

Ray thought back to his closet, the faces lined up, their expressions content, their skin smooth, their flesh forever firm. Designed to deliver pleasure.

"Pleasure is addictive. It's impossible to go back once you've experienced it. Impossible ever to enjoy the flawed fully. Comparison is the ultimate poison. In becoming addicted to the flawless, we're far more flawed than we ever were." She shifted her head on the pillow.

Ray knew, before she had even uttered the words, that he too would never, could never make love to another living person. On the level of pleasure, his companions delivered everything he could ask for, dream of. But what they could not provide was what he now craved desperately. What the past weeks had shaken to the surface of his consciousness.

In the quiet and the darkness, he reached inside himself, groping for a feeling he no longer knew the word for. A safety, perhaps, something reminiscent of the womb. Something that told him he was not alone, that he was not adrift. That it mattered, that something mattered. That something was still to come. That survival had not been in vain. But no matter how far he reached, how tightly he clung to the hand that held his, he could not find it.

Each of them slept alone.

VI

"**I** have an idea."

Allegra, who had just sat down opposite Ray at the bright green table in the hotel breakfast room, pulled in her chair and looked at him inquiringly in response to his promising greeting. She was wearing a dark cornflower blue jumpsuit, with a golden belt clasped around her waist.

The room, a sticky lounge-cum-cafeteria, was largely empty, save for an androgynous silicone waiter, her hair a cherry red, who emerged occasionally, from two big steel swinging doors to wipe the tables. Ray waited until she had disappeared again into the recesses of the invisible kitchen.

It had occurred to Ray, with a sudden jolt propelling him from the twilight state between sleep and wakefulness in which he had lingered, that perhaps the problem of preserving the missing texts lay not with the storage technology but with the scanning equipment. It was one of those stinging epiphanies that thrust him into a state of quiet but frenzied action. He had slid carefully but quickly out of Allegra's room, hurriedly dressed, and found a quiet spot to begin his research.

"You see," he explained, "the Captur software we use for scanning is Hub-issued. It was designed purposely to be able to register individual words on each scan no matter the quality. Perhaps whoever is after these documents is locking on to certain keywords and targeting them."

"I see. So, what's the alternative?"

Ray swung the screen of his tablet around so Allegra could see the image.

"A camera?" She looked back up at him, her brows furrowed.

"Not just any camera, a film camera." Ray pointed to the specifications underneath the description of the Nikon FM2.

Allegra raised her eyebrows, her eyes wide. "You mean something that captures the words as images."

"Exactly. If they are scanned and uploaded as images, perhaps we can replace the missing verses, at least temporarily." He pulled the tablet back toward him, awaiting Allegra's verdict.

She had rested her chin on her palm and was tapping her nose slowly with a forefinger.

"I like it." She sat up straight. "And I think I know where we can get what you need."

~

Ray peered up at the sign outside, trying to determine whether it really was as old and decrepit as it looked or whether it had simply been made to look so:

Herman Hernandez's Vintage Collectables & Antiques

The shop lay on the furthest outskirts of the city, facing the vast road that looped around it. Beyond the wall, at the road's edge, lay the ocean, a vast, gray, crawling expanse that mauled and spat at the thick cement. Out in its leaden depths, a series of pillars at the edge of the dome, reduced by distance to mere dashes, interrupted the horizon.

Ray drew his collar up around his neck and headed into the store.

A small bell tinkled above the door announcing their entrance. Inside, it was dark, the front window cluttered with objects that obscured the watery light from beyond. The shelves were crammed with goods the likes of which Ray had not seen since his childhood; some of which he had never seen. A wooden abacus, a rocking horse, a collection of ivory-handled cutlery in a dusty velvet-lined case, an assemblage of plastic Tupperware boxes with warped lids, and a faded suede jacket with tassels down the arms and across the yoke—fabrics and materials all banned after the war due to their depletion of environmental resources. The dim light in the room cast a dusty pallor over the otherwise colorful confusion.

The place seemed to warrant tiptoeing, much like one might in a museum, or a graveyard, afraid of what might awaken. As if in response to this thought, a mound of clothes that Ray had cast his eyes over in the far corner by the counter suddenly moved. A fuzzy head of hair, which Ray had mistaken for a mangey mink, rose to reveal an equally furry face, which broke into a wide, crinkled smile.

"Welcome, welcome! How can Herman Hernandez help you?"

The figure put out a wide, round hand that enveloped first Allegra's and then Ray's.

"Well, Mr. Hernandez," replied Allegra, taking the gamble that the man had indeed referred to himself in the third person. "We are looking for a camera."

"A camera?" He pronounced each syllable in a rich, musical accent. He pulled at the walrus-like mustache that hung over his lip. "Any particular kind?"

"Ideally, a Nikon FM2." Ray placed his hands hopefully on the glass counter, eyeing the jumble of what seemed to be ink pots and printer cartridges in old margarine boxes under the pane.

"The Nikon FM2…" The man frowned, bringing together his bushy brows. "Haven't seen one of those in many years…. It is specifically a film camera you are after?"

"Yes, I suppose any film camera would do. So long as you have the developing equipment."

A smile broke out again behind the mask of hair. "In that case, friend, Herman has just the thing you need."

When he emerged from the back of his shop, the man was shuffling under the weight of an armful of instruments, which he lay down with a clatter onto the countertop. One by one, he set them upright, and with the relish of an art dealer, he sprang into a musical and animated explanation of each.

Much like the development of a child in the womb, developing photographs requires complete darkness. Ray had not needed to give the excuse of the un-closable gap in his blinds; they made their way directly, naturally, to Allegra's room.

She cleared the dressing table of the bottles and brushes, and spread out each of the three books side by side. They worked silently, the only noises the sharp whispers of turning pages and the mechanical clicks of the camera.

By the time they had finished, they had used up the entire roll of thirty-six photographs, carefully capturing a selection of twelve of the missing sections from each of the books.

"We should use another roll, just in case." Allegra spoke barely above a whisper. Ray nodded, and slotted in a new roll of film.

Closing the books with a heavy thud once the second roll was filled, they laid out their instruments; the rubber gloves, the film reel, the scissors, the thermometer, the chemicals in amber glass to protect them from over-exposure, and from which they poured precise amounts into tall measuring tubes, and a round black plastic container, which Herman had explained was the "developer tank," the light-tight seal of which he assured them was still fully intact.

Ray sat down at the dressing table and pulled on the violet gloves, feeling their powdery insides against his palms.

"Lights?" he whispered.

Allegra swiped her finger over the brightness dial and extinguished all the bulbs in the room. Next, she pressed the button on the bedside controls and drew the blinds completely closed. The room slid into darkness.

Delicately, navigating his way around the carefully arranged instruments, Ray threaded the film into the reel. His eyes gradually became accustomed to the shadows. He worked quicker, feeding the spool of acetate into the reel, before slotting it into the developer, screwing on the lid tight.

"Lights," he repeated. His eyes stung in the sudden brightness.

They poured the chemicals one by one into the tank, agitating each for the required thirty seconds, as Herman Hernandez had eagerly explained. After the final chemical solution had been poured, shaken gently, and poured out again, they ran the tank under the bathroom tap.

The acute concentration that had abated Ray's nerves vanished, and he felt his fingers tremble as he extracted the film reel from the plastic tank. They had followed Herman's instructions diligently. With a small sponge that Herman had thrown in for free, Ray dabbed the water droplets off the dark, sepia film, and hung them to dry.

"How long did he say they needed?" Allegra asked him.

"A couple of hours," he replied, the edge of anticipation clear in his voice.

They waited. Ray on the chair, scrolling through emails on his tablet, Allegra lying on her back on the bed, her tablet raised above her. She seemed, from the glimpse Ray caught of the screen, to be reading a manuscript in a language he did not recognize.

It had not been difficult to institute English as the global language of communication. The correlation between wealth and knowledge of Romance languages was a strong one by the turn of the year 2030, and those areas that had been hardest hit by the natural and man-made destruction were largely impoverished. Life had been cheaper there, it seemed. Technology also helped the viral spread of the language, meaning even those who had escaped from areas where English was never spoken were exposed to it through the establishment of the global Hubs, and the online systems to which everyone everywhere was now linked. There were, of course, those who bemoaned the loss of diversity in the lingosphere. But the risks were simply too great, they had been told. Conflicts were born out of misunderstanding. No one ever mentioned that perhaps the greatest misunderstandings took place in silence.

The minutes passed by at an agonizing rate. Ray resisted the urge to pace in and out of the bathroom, rhythmically checking the films. The beeper he had set on his tablet finally chimed, cutting through the inertia that had seeped its way into his consciousness.

He leapt to his feet, Allegra close behind him. Delicately, he unclipped the film and held each end between pinched fingers, his arms outstretched, peering at the amber squares.

His heart sank, dragging his windpipe with it. He turned the strip over, examining it from behind, then switched the ends to opposite hands.

"I don't…understand."

Allegra was waiting behind him, peering over his shoulder. "Bring it into the bedroom." She pressed the button to draw open the blinds. "Can I see?"

Ray handed her the strip, which curled limply at the edges in a wistful attempt to wrap itself back into its original coil. She took it to the window, stretching it out against the glass.

"What on earth?" She peered at it closely. "We followed all the instructions?" She turned her head over her shoulder to Ray, who was standing at the foot of the bed.

"To the letter." The color had drained from his face.

"We must have done something wrong," she said, shaking her head and looking back at the strip splayed across the glass. "We have to try the other film." She lowered her arms, laying the film on the dressing table.

With a grim determination, Ray sat down again and pulled on the rubber gloves. He nodded to Allegra, who dimmed the lights. They were quicker this time, but cautious, double-checking every detail. Ray hung the second film in the bathroom and returned to the bedroom to meet the dread of the second wait.

This time, Ray waited outside, pacing the corridor halls. At one point, he made his way to the cafeteria with the loose intention of getting a coffee, but changed his mind at the door, the creeping nausea in his stomach threatening to put up a fight with anything he ingested.

He avoided checking his watch for fear that it would only make the time go slower. When it finally beeped, and he made his way quickly back up to their floor, he found Allegra sitting outside the door, her stockinged toes digging into the carpet, her tablet discarded beside her, evidently unable to bear the wait inside either.

She swiped her finger over the lock and pushed open the door.

This time, Allegra unclipped the film. Without looking at it, she took it back to the window. She handed Ray one end. Together they pulled the film straight and lay it against the glass.

Neither of them spoke, though the dismay that hung in the air between them was palpable.

"I don't get it, how…?"

Just as with the first film, the squares before them through which the dull late afternoon light shone were empty. The faint blur of the edges of the books' pages were visible, but the words that they had tried to capture, the words which had disappeared from all digital versions of the texts, were gone.

"We took seventy-two photographs, no scanning equipment, nothing digital involved, not even a battery… It makes no sense." Ray turned to Allegra. "Where are these words going?" His eyes were wide, searching, as if somewhere in her face he might find the answer.

"Where are they going…?" she repeated quietly, walking slowly to the bed. She sat down heavily, her eyes on the film that had fluttered from their hands to the floor, discarded, empty, like a shed snakeskin. "Where…? Yet another question."

They fell into silence for what must have been an hour. Bewildered, vexed, quiet, they sat as the setting sun drenched the room in a fiery red, turning every other color a shade of brown.

"We should tell Fielding." Ray finally broke the silence. "He's the last person I want to tell, but this is important. It means it's not the scanning equipment. At least we learned something from this…" He waved his hand at the film, now cutting a distended brown shadow on the floor.

Allegra nodded.

Ray reached for his tablet. It buzzed, suddenly, making him almost drop it. It was ringing, an undisclosed number. Ray paused, and looked up at Allegra. She stared at him. He swiped his finger across the screen.

"Ray?" came the barking voice at the other end of the line. "Ray, it's Marshall Fielding."

"Fielding, I was just about to…"

"I need you to come in immediately. Bring the Doc. But do not, I repeat, do not use your civilian lines to contact each other."

"Our civilian lines?" Ray repeated. Allegra gave him a confused look.

"Shit's really hit the fan. I need you to come in now." Ray was about to ask what had happened, but the line clicked, and the call fell dead. A pulse of dread surged between his temples.

"We need to go," he said.

Allegra was already reaching for her coat.

VII

"You're going to have to wear these." Fielding thrust what looked like two fluorescent boiler suits in Ray and Allegra's direction.

He had met them at the stairs to the basement of the Prognostics Department, a series of storage facilities that had been repurposed as temporary archives during the ongoing investigation. The shelves of the vast halls had been filled with copies of every book related, even tangentially, to religion from every zone, and when the shelves were crammed, the transport teams had taken to piling them on the floor instead.

Towers of books reached up from the rough concrete either side of the thin walkways between the shelves. Ray could see them through the thick, translucent, crinkled plastic sheets that had been hung before the glass doors to the storage areas. The interlocking talons of the biohazard symbols emblazoned on them in a waspish black and yellow seemed to glow with a throbbing fluorescence.

Inside was abuzz with similarly clad and masked figures, who were packaging books and papers into clear boxes, and stacking them into new piles.

"It seems the attack occurred last night." Fielding was talking to them over his shoulder as he led them toward some shelves at the far end of the first hall, which the hazmat-clad crew had not yet reached.

He stopped abruptly, snatching a book from the shelf. Ray caught a glimpse of the title, *Exegetica: Biblical Exegesis from the Qumran Texts.*

The book fell open in Fielding's palms, its spine crackling. He turned to them, brandishing the open book before their faces like a police badge.

"See."

Ray looked from the page to Fielding to Allegra. Her shocked expression matched his. Fielding flipped through the pages rapidly.

Every single one was the same.

Fielding tossed the book on a table behind him and pulled down another. *Tanakh Epistemology*. He flipped through the pages, which whipped across their vision like an old movie reel, constructing a black and white horror. Except that there was no black. Every single page was white.

"They're all blank?" Allegra asked, taking down a book herself.

"Every single fucking one." Fielding cast the book aside on the table and picked up another, and another, flipping and throwing, until the table surface was covered.

"How? How is this possible?" Ray broke through his dumbfounded stupor.

"Current theory is a viral agent that targets the chemical compounds of the ink. Hence the gear." He gestured toward their suits. "They're taking samples off for testing now." He stared out at the hall, filled with silent, fluorescent movement.

"It gets worse." His voice was muffled through his mask, but his tone was still clear; the stinging, personal offense as though his own home had been raided, his own personal documents defiled.

He led them into an adjoining room, smaller, filled with glass cases. There were fewer people in this one. They worked much slower, with meticulous movements.

"Manuscripts…" said Allegra, under her breath. She walked over to a case, peering at the digital labels beneath each of the open books, their dry, time-tinged pages staring blindly, mutely back up at her. She walked swiftly along the case, scanning each leather-bound volume, each outstretched scroll.

Ray and Fielding stood, watching her. She examined every single case, the same set expression across her eyes and brows—fixed, discerning. She said nothing as she walked back to the pair still standing near the first case.

Ray turned to Fielding. "We have something we need to show you, too."

~

The meeting they were summoned to did not take place in the room down the corridor from Fielding's office. It did not take place in the Department of Prognostication at all. They were sitting instead in the bowels of a huge, circular auditorium that filled an entire level of the Freedom Point Parliament building across the square.

In the center of the room, around a wide white table, sat the president, two of her advisors, the head of Prognostics, Fielding, and the directors of each of the Hub head offices. Around them, in concentric circles, more officials sat behind extending rings of desktops, equipped with in-built microphones, cameras, and screens that automatically showed the face of whoever was speaking.

Ray and Allegra were sitting in the fifth of the seven rings. The outer circles were not quite full, and the seats on either side of them were empty. The colorful heads that cascaded down before them looked sickly in the yellow of the overhead lights.

Fielding had stood, tense, repeatedly running his hand through his hair. His smile, forced, seemed to only hover over his mouth. He cleared his throat roughly, and began his summary.

The first wave of attacks had started with the removal of sections from three primary texts, he reminded the assembly: the Tanakh, also known as the Torah, the Hebrew Bible, or the Old Testament; the Bible, or the

New Testament; and the Quran. The attack had targeted digital copies of these texts in all languages. Missing sections were found to relate to violence.

At this point the president asked a question. Her face sprang to life on Ray's screen in the same crisp detail that he had seen her address the crowds in the square mere hours ago, her bottom lip moving deliberately, as though being pulled by a string. What had felt like a torrid, feverish nightmare then had taken on the dreamlike quality now of distance in Ray's mind, a scene from another life, another's life.

No, had been Fielding's answer. At no point during this, or any phase, had there been an overt message or a set of demands. At present, there was no identifiable source for these attacks, though they had teams working night and day to pin down a target.

The second wave, he continued, had taken out all references in secondary texts—supplementary and explanatory materials—relating to these verses. At this point, he reassured the president, precautions had been taken, and under the guidance of a Lit Hub expert all remaining files were being transferred to the Freedom Point network. Ray felt the skin on the back of his neck prickle. It was then, however, while the transfer was in progress, that large portions of the primary texts—the figure now stood at least sixty-five percent—had been deleted from the digital archives. This included any reference to, Fielding looked at his notes, gender or other classifiers.

Fielding shifted his weight on his feet and ran his hand through his hair again.

It was last night, he informed the assembly, that a new and unprecedented development had taken place: A third attack was made on both soft and hard copies of the secondary texts. He paused. All of which, he revealed, had been wiped.

A ripple ran around the room, hisses and whispers of shock.

It had also been brought to his attention, Fielding continued, that it was not only hard copies but also non-digitized images of hard copies that were wiped. They were looking at a number of possibilities in addition to a viral attack, including a chemical agent released into the archives, possibly through the ventilation systems. The department was, of course, being swept for indicators, he assured the room, and the staff thoroughly questioned.

"Was it possible to say whether this attack was confined only to these three texts and their associated literature?" The president's face was grim as she directed this question at Fielding. Ray saw him swallow and clench his jaw on the screen before him.

"No, ma'am. I cannot say for sure."

There was a long, heavy pause before Fielding continued. Despite himself, Ray felt a flicker of sympathy for the man, his discomfort resonating through the screen, the personal weight of responsibility he seemed to bear echoing in his voice.

They were now relocating the primary texts to a maximum security location, and were investigating what seemed to have been a breach in the Prognostics basement security system.

"Given the seriousness and scope of the situation, we felt the time was right to inform Parliament, and initiate a city-wide response. We're calling this a Code Scarlet." Fielding ran a hand across his jaw.

The president leaned forward in her chair, her elbows resting on the table, her hands clasped, her chin propped on her extended thumbs.

The woman next to her spoke, her face flashing up onto the screens around the room, her name and title appearing in stark white letters beneath. Her face was severe, as though drawn entirely with straight lines. Her lips were purple, and her eyeshadow the color of slate.

"This breach, if not contained, could be lethal to life as we know it. Who knows what is being done with these missing texts, how they are being read, and by whom."

"Is it a message? A threat?" another woman chimed, her salmon hair offsetting her deep brown skin.

A flurry of voices joined the growing clamor.

"And who knows what they could target next! Our entire archives are at risk. Any piece of information could be erased!"

"And the archiving is not even complete…" Another face flashed on the screen, an older man his age belied by the wrinkled skin of his neck and barely disguised by his unnaturally swollen shiny cheeks and lips and his jet-black hair. He had lowered his face to the microphone, so it swelled across the screen. "Our systems hacked, words disappearing from print, information vanishing into the ether…" He waved his hands before the screen.

"This undermines our entire system! Our entire way of life! A repeat of '35." A man's voice, the twang of his accent apparent through his stress on certain consonants, echoed loudly.

"No, this is worse," another voice shouted back above the increasing rumble of panic. "Worse than '35 and worse than the Burn!"

"We will be forced back into the age of paper and ink, of vulnerability, of chaos!"

"This is chaos!"

Another ripple ran around the room, tense, fearful. People were standing. Palms slammed against surfaces. Voices threatened to rise further. The screen flashed from face to face as fear stretched its tentacles around the room.

"Whatever this is," the president's voice, calm but sharp, cut the murmuring dead. "I have full faith that the investigation team will get to the bottom of it. Panic and fear are pre-war relics. Do not stoop to such insecurities. We are the fortunate recipients of a legacy of technology that surpasses anything humankind has ever known, and we will restore our equilibrium and our peace." Her words rang out through the microphones, steel-like, ardent. She allowed the silence to settle before she began again.

"What we need now, from you, our dedicated protectors of freedom, is help. Not fear, nor scaremongering. Help. If there are any constructive comments or questions from the floor, now is your chance to voice them."

She looked pointedly around the room, her gaze lingering on those downturned faces that had so avidly contributed to the whispers.

"I have a question." The screen switched to a young woman, her face barely visible beneath the large frames of her glasses. "Have audio versions of these books also been affected?"

The president looked swiftly to Fielding, whose face showed a mixture of both relief and discomfort. "We will have a team investigate the audio archives immediately."

"There you are," said the president, her shoulders relaxing. "Perhaps there is a solution to this mess right within our reach."

~

Ray, Allegra, and Fielding stood huddled around the table. A tablet lay in the middle, its screen black except for the microphone icon and a progress bar that counted down the seconds.

The audio file hissed quietly, spitting out the white noise that had become synonymous with silence, but which, as it played from the digital file over the speakers in Fielding's office, had never sounded louder. They jumped as the voice returned.

We offered the trust to the heavens and the earth and the mountains, but they refused to carry it and were afraid of doing so; but the human carried it.

Fielding stopped the file, and a new silence descended on the office.

"It's the same. All the secondary texts are gone. Primary texts have sections missing. And now the audio is missing. They've got into everything. Everything."

"Tapes? Do we try cassette tapes?" Ray asked.

"I'll get a team on it. But at this point…I think we know the results."

Fielding's voice was flat and heavy, like a weight that descended upon the room every time he spoke. A shudder of fear ran through Ray's chest. As much as he detested the man, it was one thing for Ray to feel defeated, it was another for Fielding to look so beaten.

Ray swallowed. He turned to Allegra. "Where else would these texts be kept? We have to find a sustainable source to replace our archives. If this continues, who knows where it will end." He felt a strange, inexplicable frenzy rise in him, as though perhaps Fielding's absence of verve had inspired his own. "We could be left without any books at all."

Allegra was quiet. She seemed to be neither fearful nor impassioned in response to the recent developments. Instead, she appeared to be consumed by a quiet curiosity, blanketed in a deep state of rumination.

"What you are looking for is the repository of knowledge before the internet, before even books." She spoke in a distant voice.

"Yes," replied Ray, relieved that she had a response.

"The mind, or the heart, as it was then referred to, was the original library. Before words were written, they were memorized. What you're looking for are minds."

"Tell me you know where we can find them." Ray was standing, his hand now on Allegra's shoulder, beseeching.

"I do."

PART III

While violence was rampant between all faiths during the early years of the conflict, not all adherents of the Abrahamic traditions ascribed to a homicidal understanding of their texts. There were those who adhered to a spiritual interpretation, however difficult that was to derive. But despite their search for peace within their pages, this minority found themselves in the unique position of becoming universal enemies. On one side, they were branded "fanatics" on account of their adherence to scripture in any form. On the other, they were branded "traitors" and "heretics" for daring to question a literal reading of the sacred. By both sides, their eradication was sought. All the while, chemical, biological, and digital warfare raged, increasingly indiscriminate.

In the hushed deliberations of these communities concerning their fate—Muslims, Christians, and Jews—a theme recurred. At first, it was a murmur, a pondering. Then, as the violence grew, it became an idea. Finally, it became a plan.

"The Messiah," it was said, "will descend on the White Tower, east of Damascus."

And it was to Damascus they fled.

They may have each understood the messianic arrival differently, but their anticipation was equally intense. The walls of the Old City had been destroyed by much of the violence, but the basic infrastructure remained intact. It is a curious fact of war that leaders are reluctant to destroy places of beauty. After all, when they conquer enemy lands, they must have somewhere to live. Damascus, the Old City in particular, was not just beautiful—with its rich sandstone buildings, winding alleys, jasmine flowers, and rose domes—it was also steeped in history. It was the oldest continually inhabited city on earth, never abandoned, never empty, never completely destroyed.

The violence that had gripped Damascus, and the entire region, long before the war of '33, had wiped out many of the original inhabitants. Those who survived had largely fled. By the time the influx of fleeing believers had begun, only a quarter of the city's original inhabitants remained. And for the most part, they too were waiting.

The first thing the fleeing communities did upon arrival was to rebuild the city walls, thick and high, which swung around it in a wide oval, their edges meeting at the Citadel originally built in the eleventh century, repurposed now as a place of neutral gatherings.

The next was to cover the winding alleys, courtyards, and straight Roman streets in arched roofs of corrugated iron, in the style of the main souk, the Hamidiyeh, through which shafts of sunlight spilled in via bullet holes that gave one the sense, staring up at it, of looking at the stars.

Only one courtyard was left unroofed: that of the Grand Mosque, in part out of practicality, for the logistics of such a task were insurmountable, but also, partly, out of faith, the belief that somehow anyone entering the sacred space—from people to pigeons—would be protected. Raised from the ground in the Iron Age as an Aramaean temple, the Grand Mosque had seen and sheltered those who had come to worship in the name of Hadad, Jupiter, and the God of Abraham. Names that now did not matter. All those who stepped inside were safe.

Inhabitants of this walled community, along with their deep spirituality, brought with them an asceticism, a love for tradition, a yearning for the unadulterated. Technology was an unnatural thing, a distraction from the organic, the pure. Except where necessity dictated, they largely shunned the contraptions and contrivances of modern technology. They lived frugally, they farmed at night in the wide stretches of abandoned land to the southeast. Where possible, they lived in the past, one constructed only from peaceful memories, free of the realities even their own histories described.

Each community lived side by side, deciding they had more in common with each other than with the religious namesakes they had fled from. Church bells, sounded as calls to prayer, rang from minarets, and the streets, speckled with light, were filled with an eclectic array of religious garbs. Separately they worshiped, side by side they lived. Together, in the City of the Messiah, they waited.

Messiah City had not been unique in its concept. Simultaneous to its burgeoning as a sanctuary for those of the Abrahamic faiths, the city of Varanasi also swelled with an influx of Hindus, Sikhs, Buddhists, and Jains of a spiritual persuasion. They fortified the area and swore binding oaths to protect one another against those forces—religious and anti-religious—who sought their eradication. It was with forty days of mourning that those in Messiah City erected a monument to all those who had died in the missile attack that struck Varanasi, and they welcomed the few gaunt and struggling survivors into their own walls. Every year, upon the anniversary of the news of their sister city's fate, they laid a wreath of Damask roses at the foot of the monument, raised their hands in supplication for the departed souls, and prayed for the health and peace of their own sacred home.

The new powers who took charge of the rest of the world after 2040 were reluctant to dismantle this haven of religious peace—not for any ideological reasons, although doing so would have smacked of hypocrisy when done under the auspices of "freedom." They were reluctant simply because they did not wish to inflame the kind of religious tensions that had contributed to so much of the violence in the early years of the conflict. Nor, however, did they wish to leave this city unmonitored. While the spokesmen and women of Messiah City assured Freedom Parliament of their absolute and undying commitment to peace, the city's existence, with its aversion to technology and its insistence on tradition, posed a threat to their new way of life. A compromise was reached. All inhabitants of the city were to be registered and documented and were neither allowed to leave nor enter without prior approval. In such a way, this microcosm of unpredictability could be contained, and its impact, if any, predicted.

~

Ray, Allegra, and Fielding arrived by helicopter; large, black, with four horizontal propellers and no windows save for the pilot's, which was made from the same material as the dome over Freedom Point.

The journey had been loud; the three of them had been silent. The whirring of the propellers had pounded against Ray's eardrums, despite the thick protectors they each wore. The constant roar and the pressure against the sides of his head isolated him in a padded room of noise, which seemed only to amplify the voices in his head.

Why was this happening? Why now? Why these texts? And why was any of this important?

It was this final question that whirred almost as loud as the blades, and the answer was even louder. A whirring he could not stop, that had hummed in the back of his mind for years, that had grown to a deafening pitch the moment he had seen the first blank space struck across a page where words had once been. It was the blip in the interstellar radio waves that once held the promise of life, a glimmer along the blackness of the ocean floor. It made his insides flutter. It made him want to gasp for breath, strain his eyes for something more. It was the ultimate betrayal of the status quo, the treasonous act of excitement in the face of a threat, the guilt-ridden delight in watching a catastrophe play out. It was at once the reason why people had crawled past highway accidents, eager for a glimpse, and why people had once looked for life beyond their own planet. And just as such people could never admit to wanting to look, Ray could not admit to wanting, desperately, to see what would unfold.

Ray looked over to Allegra, strapped against the opposite bench in the belly of the roaring metal beast. Her eyes were closed, her hair clamped to her head by the earphones. She swayed, as he did, with the jolting motion of the craft. Her lashes cut a thin line between the lids of her eyes.

Ray recalled the package that had awaited him on the doorstep of his hotel room the night before their departure, a mere twelve hours ago. He had dragged it in with a sickening sense of shame and foreboding, hopeful that no other guests had seen it, though sure that he was not alone in receiving such a package. He had not expected such a delivery in Freedom Point, and yet he knew he should not have been surprised to see it.

It was with a curiosity devoid of any level of excitement that he peeled back the flap to reveal the face. The level of detail was alarming. Though he knew the companies were careful never to replicate the features of recent predicted interests for fear of their clients freezing at the sight of them, it was always obvious who they were designed to mirror. The face before him was smooth, the hair long and dark, and the cupid's bow deep. The eyes had been closed. He had stared at it for a long time. And then, closing the flap, he had opened the door, and left the package outside.

The helicopter landed heavily. They clambered out and ran, heads bowed, ducking through the gray dust kicked up in a whirl around them.

Old Damascus had seven gates, each of which was meticulously restored, but only two of which were in use: Bab al-Faraj, The Gate of Deliverance, near the northeast corner of the citadel, which acted as the main checkpoint in and out of Messiah City; and Bab Sharqi, the Eastern Gate, the only Roman gate still standing before the new settlers arrived. It was through this gate that the city dwellers accessed the wide expanses of wilderness beyond the eastern walls that they had painstakingly cultivated by lantern light. And it was through this gate that the trio from Freedom Point arrived.

The minaret beside the gate was tall, emerald tipped, illuminated by soft, skyward-facing floodlights. The guards, assigned by Freedom Point, checked their passes, scanned their irises, and took their fingerchip readings on blinking screens. One of them, a man with unfortunate features, attempted to bark questions at them and was quickly silenced by Fielding, who flashed his pass in their faces, reminding them exactly who they were talking to and the consequences of taking such a tone.

Though they had arrived at night, the air was hot and dry, as if radiating up from the earth itself. Ray ran his finger around his cravat. His shirt had stuck to his back and sides from the hard seats in the helicopter. His head spun, his ears throbbed from having been so tightly compressed, and his desperation to lie down somewhere quiet overwhelmed the relentless churning in his stomach at the thought of what would meet them on the other side of the walls that now loomed over them.

A small door in the vast iron gates swung slowly inwards. A face peered out.

"Welcome!" A woman stepped out of the door into the concrete confines of the checkpoint. The guards cast her threatening looks as though daring her to come out any farther.

Her hair was dark, splayed in a chaos of curls about her round face, her skin a dark olive. "Welcome to the City of the Messiah!"

She shook their hands eagerly, scanning their faces as though to perform whatever checks a tablet might have done, though what she was looking for was unclear. "My name is Rebekah. I've been assigned as your guide."

Ray saw Fielding raise an eyebrow at the woman's appearance. She was wearing a pair of loose linen pants, and a faded striped tunic cut of similar cloth. Her feet were clad in dusty, brown leather sandals. Ray stumbled over his own introduction, surprised by both her attire and indeed her presence. He was not sure what he had expected, but he certainly hadn't expected a cheerful young woman dressed in flowing garb.

One by one they followed her through the door, and into the walls of the city. Behind them, the helicopter rose from the field and dragged itself away through the night. Ray breathed a low sigh of relief as, like a blanket over a body, a quietness fell over them. He took in his surroundings. They stood at the side of a road, which swung away from them in both directions. It was dusty, as though the largely desertified lands beyond the city waged a constant battle for entrance. The buildings were sandstone, and the road was dotted with palms, which swayed sleepily, their leaves rustling.

"At night," Rebekah was telling them, "we open the roofs. It's important to see the sky." They looked up. The corrugated iron arches that stretched over the streets had been pulled back, like eyelids, gaping half-open toward the sky, spattered with stars. She led them to a small carriage, drawn by a shiny-eyed mule, atop of which sat an elderly man, with an equally wide smile, who greeted them with a series of energetic nods as they clambered in.

Fielding, aghast, was the last to climb in, taking his seat heavily next to Ray with a look of profound disgust. Flustered by their mode of transport and the smiling command Rebekah had taken, he cleared his throat and began his attempt to reassert control of the situation.

"Where is it you're taking us, uh… Rachel, was it?"

Rebekah, from the seat next to the driver, looked back at them cheerfully. "Rebekah," she reminded him. "I'm sorry, I should have told you, we don't get many visitors! We're headed to the Citadel first to get you settled in. We've arranged the meetings you requested for tomorrow morning. It's late here, I'm afraid. And we've had a bit of a…" A shadow of concern suddenly fell across her face. "Well… I think it's best if you hear it from the elders in your meeting tomorrow." She smiled again, not artificially, Ray noticed, but with an unexpected warmth, which made him feel at once at ease and slightly uncomfortable, as though she had somehow seen photographs of him as a child.

They rode quietly through the half-hooded streets, the lights from the sandstone houses warm and rich, crisscrossing their beams across the narrow roads, through which no pod, Ray realized, could ever have fit. Ignoring the bumping of Fielding's arm against his own, he breathed deeply. There seemed, when he listened intently, to be a faint singing, just audible above the rumble of the wheels and the rhythmic clatter of hooves.

Eventually, the carriage pulled up outside the Citadel–tall, a patchwork of stones, each as big as a human, illuminated dimly by the floor lights that cast their beams upwards toward the ancient battlements. From its yawning doorway, a tall, slender woman walked toward them with a willowy grace. Her shawl, wrapped loosely around her neck, and her long tunic-like robe were dyed what looked like, in the faint light, to be a soft moss green, which both contrasted with and complemented the deep, dark shade of her skin. Her eyes shone, as if illuminated by a light of their own.

"This is the Custodian of the Citadel." Rebekah stood smiling next to the woman, who also shook each of their hands, clasping them in her own. "I leave you in her care until morning."

"My name is Elaina. Welcome to Messiah City, to our home." Her voice was deep, like an underground stream. She, like Rebekah, looked long at each of their faces—again, Ray felt at once at home, and entirely foreign. She turned to walk through the huge arched doorways. "Your rooms have been prepared. Your meetings will take place after dawn, whilst the sun is still gentle. Until then, you must rest."

The door creaked as it swung open, revealing, slowly, the astonishing chamber within. The stone pillars that held up the high ceiling were intricately carved, such that each appeared to tell a story. Their branches met each other in sweeping arches, forming a canopy above them that encircled a central latticed dome through which starlight shone in intersecting slivers. Their footsteps echoed on the stone floors as they followed Elaina, who glided up a staircase at the far end of the hall.

Their rooms, though narrow, were also high-ceilinged, with tall windows at the far end, the wooden shutters of which were wide open. Ray, having bid good night to Allegra and Fielding, and having watched the willowy woman float back down the staircase, closed his door quietly behind him.

On the low bed next to which flickered an elegant lantern, a set of clothes had been laid out neatly—a long tunic and a simple suit. He bent to touch them, feeling the soft linen fabric between his fingers. They seemed to be the color of tree bark and sand.

Ray walked quietly to the window and leaned against the sill. Creeping in was the faint smell of jasmine, which wafted past him with each breath of night air. With their covers thrown back he could trace the narrow streets, lit by faint orange streetlamps. The houses were built in a chaotic confusion, the way in which many old cities once were, piled on top of one another, at varying heights and breadths, interspersed with church towers and minarets, domes, and steeples.

From this height, he could make out the small shapes of people milling through the streets, and he started to pick out shop fronts and cafes by the pools of light with which they flooded the streets before them. But the more he looked, the more Ray realized that the movement was not coming from the streets alone but from the rooftops. Each of the buildings before him, he realized, was roofed with a flat surface upon which its inhabitants had built gardens. Now that he focused, he could pick out the dense foliage, the specks of white in among what must have been jasmine bushes, the fruit trees swaying gently in the night breeze.

He slid off his shoes and socks and felt the cold tiles of the floor bite at his feet. He poured himself water from a large jug and drank, feeling the crisp fluid funnel down inside him. There was a bowl of fruit, figs he recalled, which he had not seen since he was a child and had never eaten. Some were a ruddy purple, others a bright yellow-green. He bit into a purple one, the skin tight, faintly prickly, the flesh inside soft, and slightly sweet.

He picked up another and examined it, wondering if he had ever tasted anything like it. The green ones were smaller, sweeter, equally as fragrant, and seemed to fill him quickly. It was only now, in the reassuring and unexpected calm of his surroundings, that he realized how hungry he had been.

He undressed slowly and dipped his hands in the large copper bowl of rippling water at his bedside. He ran his hands down his face and trickled droplets down his spine, allowing the night air to cool and dry them. Then, he slid on the tunic and climbed beneath the thin covers.

The room was quiet, as though the stone had absorbed the noise even of his own breathing. And yet, as he fell asleep, it occurred to Ray that from somewhere he could still hear singing.

~

The breeze that carried the dawn chorus of calls to prayer in through Ray's window was mellow. He washed his face in the large copper bowl, banishing the last dregs of sleep, and changed into the clothes that had been laid out on the bed.

"So that you won't attract unnecessary eyes," Rebekah had said, with her impenetrable air of disarming warmth.

When he pulled open his bedroom door, Ray noticed Allegra and Fielding already standing in the corridor.

"Good morning," said Allegra, quietly as though not to wake the stone. She was dressed in a tunic suit much like his, except hers was a light blue. She had a long linen scarf wrapped about her shoulders.

"Good morning," Ray replied. Fielding, who was jabbing a finger tensely at his tablet, clearly uncooperative, looked up briefly, and grunted in Ray's direction. He, to Ray's surprise, was dressed in the suit he had worn yesterday, a dark teal with mustard trim.

Allegra nodded toward Ray's attire. "When in Rome," she smiled. Ray smiled back.

"Rome was destroyed a long time ago," said Fielding, his voice contemptuous. He leaned toward them. "Don't be fooled by the hippy facade. It's this lot that started the whole fucking thing back in '33," he snarled in a low voice. It finally dawned on Ray, coldly and heavily, the reason Fielding had accompanied them on this mission. It had struck him as odd that Fielding was assigned to the trip. Anyone from Prognostics could have accompanied them and filled in a report. Fielding, it was now clear, was on a fact-finding mission of his own.

"I'm afraid you won't have much luck with electronics in the Citadel," came a smooth voice from behind them. Elaina was standing at the top of the stairs. She placed her hand on the stone. "These walls were designed to keep things out."

Fielding flashed her a full-toothed smile, oddly sharp around the edges. "I'm going to need to talk to the governing committee, your... leaders." The condescension in his voice broke through only slightly with this final word.

"Of course. Everything has been arranged." The Custodian, dressed today in clothes the color of clay, either did not notice his tone or chose not to. "But first you must eat. Please, follow me."

They were fed at a long wooden table in a room decorated with lattice walls through which lanterns shone. Sitting on high-backed chairs, they drank the strong dark tea and ate from the selection of dried fruits while also enjoying bread dipped in rich olive oil. From time to time, Ray cast a glance at Allegra, who seemed more than ever to be held captive by some ongoing contemplation, emerging every so often only to exchange a few words with him. Fielding was still hammering at his tablet.

"You are here, I understand, to hear the recitations of sacred texts." Elaina, whom no one had noticed re-enter the room, was standing in the doorway speaking. "There is something I must ask of you."

"What is that?" asked Fielding, sharply.

Elaina sat down slowly at the table. "You see, not long ago, the words from many of our books started disappearing. In a matter of days, many of them were left entirely blank."

"Yes, we know. That's why we are here. This has become a global phenomenon." Fielding seemed agitated by the apparent uselessness of this information.

Sensing the potential offense, Ray turned to Elaina. "We were hoping that in order to preserve these texts, we might record them being read from memory. We understand that the preservation of oral transmission methods here is encouraged."

"Indeed it is, but what you must understand is that this disappearance has unsettled many in our community. It has been interpreted by some as a sign of the ends of time."

"The ends of time?" Fielding scoffed.

"Yes," replied Elaina, again ignoring his tone. "As such, I would ask you to be sensitive to the communities here. I realize that beyond these walls sensibilities such as ours are not viewed favorably, but this is our way of life."

Though her tone was gentle, and her voice fluid, her message was clear. Fielding cleared his throat, gave her a sharp nod, and returned to his tablet.

Rebekah, arriving with the same driver, whom they later discovered was her uncle, cheerfully shepherded Ray and Allegra out of the Citadel walls and into the courtyard. Fielding had stayed behind to conduct his own meetings.

Dawn was breaking overhead; the sky was tinged a pale pink. As they rode into the increasingly narrow streets, like the closing petals of a great flower overhead, the arched iron ceilings drew shut, blotting out the steadily brightening rays of the morning. The streets, now lit by lamps and windows, narrowed even further in on themselves.

For so early in the day, there was a surprising number of people strolling through the streets. The carriage weaved its way around them, the carts of fruit and vegetables, and the shop fronts that had spilled their wares out onto small patches of the street. The people, Ray noticed, were dressed in muted tones. Browns, greens, blues, creams, and sands, a far cry from the technicolor arrays of Freedom Point or even of his own home. They seemed somehow soft, cheerful, despite their somewhat shriveled frames, bony shoulders, and hollow cheeks.

"Food is a challenge here," Rebecca commented, as though intuiting Ray's thoughts. "We grow our own but feeding a nation with only a few fields and rooftop gardens is difficult."

"What do you do for medicine?" asked Allegra, leaning forward to talk to her.

"We rely on exchanges with Freedom Point. They were very generous with their most recent deal," Rebekah smiled. "In exchange for access to foreigners."

It did not occur to Ray, until they passed a large huddle of them waiting outside a wide fenced playground, that there was a surprisingly high number of children.

"Go forth and multiply," laughed Rebekah, catching Ray's expression. "I hear that this commandment has been largely abandoned beyond our city walls."

"I can count the number of children I've seen this year on one hand," Ray told her.

Rebekah looked at him with concern. "But surely, your nation will die out?"

The carriage was silent.

Their destination was a large building, the doorway to which was set into a black and white stone archway. A curled calligraphic inscription in a language Ray could not read spread out over the door.

"Arabic," said Allegra.

"You know Arabic?" Rebekah turned to her, pleasantly surprised.

"I have a reading knowledge only, I'm afraid. I haven't heard it spoken in many years."

"Here, most of us can speak, or at least understand, English. Of course, many grew up with it. But as part of our spiritual code, we have been committed to keeping our sacred languages alive; Arabic, Hebrew, Greek, and even Aramaic."

"How fascinating," said Allegra, looking intently back at the inscription. "House of Narrations," she translated. "You know, I've only ever read of this place in books."

"Narrations?" asked Ray, curiously.

"Yes," said Rebekah, turning to him. "*Hadith*, sayings of the Prophet Muhammad. The women here have dedicated their lives to memorizing them by heart."

"How many narrations are there?" Ray was intrigued.

"Somewhere in the region of four thousand, I believe." Rebekah pulled up the scarf around her shoulders, fixing it over her head. Allegra did the same. Ray, in the absence of a similar garment, felt conspicuously undressed, and ran his finger around his collar, unused to the breeze against his neck. They slipped off their shoes and walked through the dark green doorway into the building.

Inside was a courtyard, canopied entirely with jasmine vines, such that no iron or stone roof was needed. Any sunlight that stole its way through the leaves was dyed a dappled green. But it was not, in fact, the sight of the courtyard that met them first, but rather its sounds. Sitting on the floor in small clusters, on richly woven carpets, were groups of women of all ages, in their hundreds, clad entirely in white, their faces framed by headscarves, the shades of their skin speaking to the many parts of the world from which they had fled. In a concord of low voices, each woman was reciting—their eyes closed, concentrating. The sound vibrated through the cool air in the shady space. Ray was transfixed.

A woman who wore a blue shawl about her shoulders stood and walked forward to greet them. She held her hand to her chest as she introduced herself warmly in a stream of melodious syllables.

"This is Aminah. She is the head of the school," Rebekah translated. She and Aminah continued their exchange in Arabic. Aminah nodded, an intense expression across her face. Ray held his breath, fearful that at any moment the chance to record the words that had wondrously reappeared in the form of sounds and syllables might suddenly be withdrawn.

Rebekah smiled and nodded but turned to Ray and Allegra with a slightly nervous look across her brow. "She would like to know," she asked hesitantly, "if you believe in God?"

Ray looked at her. What would have been his usual answer did not seem like the sensible one, and yet, he certainly could not lie, profess belief in a concept the rest of the world had long ago not only lost faith in but found no space for. He swallowed.

"I believe in the universe." Beside him, Allegra had put her hand on her chest. Ray looked from her to Aminah, nodding slowly in cautious agreement. Rebekah translated.

Aminah considered Allegra's answer for a moment, her gaze gentle but scrutinizing. Then, she smiled.

"She said, that will do for now," Rebekah translated, looking relieved.

Aminah turned to the room of reciting women and called out a name that Ray did not catch. Another woman, who could not have been more than twenty, stood up and walked toward them. Though Ray could not see the outline of her body, something about the way she walked reminded him distinctly of Monica. The thought of her sent a strange, dull twinge through his chest, followed by the curious realization that she had not crossed his mind for days now.

"This is Khadija," said Rebecca, translating. "She is the school's top student. She has memorized all six books in the canon of narrations." The young woman placed her hand on her chest and bowed her head to them.

They followed Aminah and Khadija to a small room at the back of the courtyard, filled with tables and chairs. Ray placed the large black case of recording equipment on the table and unzipped it. To cover all bases, they had brought with them both wireless recording technology, as well as a cassette-based recorder of the type dating back to the era of longwave and shortwave radio, when digital recordings were still only a fantasy.

With the equipment arranged on the desk, leaving them little more than elbow room, Allegra clipped two small microphones to Khadija's tunic, then sat back next to Ray at the desk. Aminah sat behind them, her cool presence palpable, ready to catch any errors in Khadija's recitation. Two minds were always better than one, they had reasoned.

"We would like you simply to start at the beginning of the first book," Allegra told her, preparing the recording tablet.

Rebekah translated. Khadija nodded. Settling her hands, clasped, on the table before her, she closed her eyes. She breathed in deeply, as though gathering up the sounds rippling around them from the courtyard. In a crisp, clear voice, she began.

They stopped only to allow the women to pray, and to drink the tea and refreshments brought in on a silver tray. Ray's shoulders were sore from sitting, and his eyes ached from monitoring the barometers on the screen, but his sense of marvel at the fluidity of the woman's recitation did not leave him. He may not have understood a word, but the authority with which the woman recited captivated him. Strange vowels and consonants filled the air in a constant stream around him. It was almost like listening to music.

By the time they had thanked Khadija and Aminah, night had fallen. They stepped outside into the warm breath of the evening, the scent of the jasmine strong and heady around them.

It was Allegra's idea to walk back to the Citadel. "A city can only be truly experienced on foot," she had said, as she repeated Rebekah's directions back to her. The fleeting tightness that had clenched itself around Ray's chest at the prospect of a nighttime stroll in a foreign city dissipated instantly as he stepped into the narrow alley toward which Rebekah had waved them. The chatter of life rebounded off the sandstone walls around them, lanterns swayed, casting playful shadows up the crumbling walls. The air was warm, alive.

Perhaps it was the noise of the city that quelled the noise that had so long lived within him. A noise without words, but with fingers, that had clutched at his throat, at his chest—an empty noise, questions with no answers, feelings without thought. Perhaps it was the recitation that quieted it; melodious, fathomless, still ringing in his ears.

The road broadened, winding around the houses, their edges soft, so unlike the harshness he had become accustomed to. A man with a donkey pulled a cart of bobbing stacks of bread behind him, the tall, fragrant piles teetering as the cart rumbled along the road. He smiled at them, a large toothless greeting, and placed his hand on his chest. His clothes were the color of bread, his shoes worn, his expression uncomplicated. Ray smiled back, returning the gesture.

The man drew the cart to a halt, stroking the long ears of the donkey gently. Ray and Allegra stopped, wondering what had happened. He turned to them, saying something in a language that sounded like the words they had spent all day listening to. He repeated his unintelligible injunction, walking to the back of his cart.

"I think he wants to know if we'd like some bread."

Ray turned to the man, the warm, floury scent filling the street. He pulled at his empty pockets and shook his head sadly. "No money."

The man waved his hands in a dismissive gesture, his smile still wide across his face. He slid his hand into the pile and lifted off a stack of the thin, round pieces, tying them up deftly with a piece of string. He pressed the stack into Ray's arms.

Ray shook his head. "No money," he repeated. "I'm sorry." The man waved his arms again, pressing the bread against Ray's chest. The warmth permeated his clothes, spreading across his skin.

"I think he's giving them to you," Allegra whispered. She put her hand on her chest and bowed her head in thanks.

The man returned the gesture, leaving them with words they could only interpret as blessings, as he patted his donkey and the cart rumbled on. Ray watched the man disappear down the road, calling out his wares as children tripped over doorsteps to offer him coins in return for their own stacks. Allegra laughed softly, and tore off a piece, popping it into her mouth, closing her eyes in delight at the taste and texture.

They continued their walk through the streets, the bread now radiating its heat deep into Ray's chest, wrapping him in its scent. They wandered leisurely, craning their heads up, taking in the sight of the sky that had never seemed so close, as if it only hovered over the rooftops. In the distance, in the gaps between the tumbling rows of houses, they could see a minaret, illuminated at its peak, appearing and disappearing as they meandered their way toward the Citadel. As they approached, they realized that it was not one minaret they could see but three, each different in their design, one rectangular, another ornately crested. They stood over the city like guardians, keeping watch over the streets.

Just when they thought the alleys might never end, they happened upon a large open space, the sight of which came upon them like a sudden breath. They had rounded the Grand Mosque, they realized, as Rebekah had said they would, and before them stood a large stone arch, alone, bereft of whatever it had supported, but proud, nonetheless, noble in its survival, its edges crumbling.

"The gate of the Temple of Jupiter," Ray heard Allegra whisper, awed. She was walking toward it slowly. "It was built over two thousand years ago." Ray followed her. Together, they stood beneath the arch, looking up at the keystone, laid in the first century before their own era had begun. "How many lives have passed beneath this, I wonder?" Allegra asked.

Ray felt a tapping at his foot. He looked down to see a pigeon, glittery-eyed, its head cocked up toward him. It took him a second to realize he was still holding the bread that had so melded with his warmth that it felt like an extension of his own flesh. Another pigeon fluttered down and joined them. "They're hungry," he realized.

"Come." Allegra placed her hand on his arm. He felt her heat through his sleeve, as warm as the bread. Through the floury aroma, he caught the scent of almonds.

They headed over to a low stone wall spanning a courtyard next to the arch. Ray placed the bread between them. One by one they tore apart the large, warm pieces and threw them to the birds. Soon they were surrounded by flocks of pigeons, their wings whistling as they alighted on the ground before them, pecking at the pieces. Children from neighboring houses emerged, laughing at the growing throng of birds. From the corner of his eye, Ray noticed one child had perched on the wall not far from them. Her light brown hair, curly, stood out wildly around her face, her cheeks a blotchy pink. She was edging slowly along the wall toward them, tiptoeing carefully, her eyes on the cooing pigeons exploring her toes poking out of her sandals. She giggled as one pecked the shiny buckle.

"Would you like some?" Ray held out a piece of bread to her. She raised her shoulder to her cheek shyly. "Take it—it's for you," Ray reassured her. With a small, dimpled hand she took the piece of bread and tore off a large chunk. She laughed as several pigeons dove at the generous piece, and she threw another.

The wave of feeling that Ray had been aware of, ever since they had stepped into the city walls, crested against his chest, overwhelming. He put his hands in his lap, a piece of bread still between his fingers, and took in the scene; the birds, the bread, the laughter of the children, the ushering parents, the overlooking minarets, the ancient gaze of the arch. He turned to Allegra. She looked up from the pigeons at her feet. He didn't say a word, but she nodded. Ray nodded back.

As he fell asleep that night, Ray was sure he could still hear the cooing of the pigeons and the voice of Khadija reciting.

II

"This is Straight Street, also known as The Street Called Straight," Rebekah commented cheerfully, her energy somewhat overwhelming at such an early hour of the morning.

Ray rubbed his eyes dryly, and watched the scenes tumble past the cart as the dawn air, still fresh, ran its fingers across his skin. His neck tingled. The taste of dried apricots lingered at the back of his tongue as they rode through the growing dawn light and eventually into the lantern-lit darkness as the roofs closed over them.

"If I'm not mistaken, this was mentioned in the New Testament," said Allegra, also craning her neck to take in the vast sense of history that rushed past.

"*Decumanus maximus*, that's right," Rebekah smiled. "Paul is said to have stayed in a house along this road. It runs all the way from the west to the east."

Their destination, the Cathedral of Saint George, was located in the old Christian quarter, known as Bab Tuma. Rebekah's uncle turned left off Straight Street, down a smaller road, and drew the carriage to a stop outside the building. It was smaller than Ray had expected, its facade sweeping up into a triangle of stone, its angles illuminated by rows of lights hidden in its design. Above the door, with its large archway, was a marble engraving set into the sandy-colored stone.

"Saint George and the dragon," remarked Allegra. Ray looked up at the knight on the rearing steed, spear poised over the heart of the monster that lay writhing at his feet. He wondered what Freedom Point parliament would make of such an icon, particularly now in the light of recent attacks.

The hall inside was largely white, with sturdy marble pillars holding up the lofty ceilings. At the end of the church, three broad arches were built, two closed off with thick, rich red velvet curtains. It was the most vivid color Ray had seen since his arrival in the city. Into the curved top of the arches were fixed lights that gave the place a festive feel, of the warm type Ray remembered only vaguely from childhood.

The church was eerily quiet and their footsteps echoed sharply on the marble floors.

"Father Yuhanna should be here somewhere," Rebekah said, scanning the room.

Ray was tempted to sit down on one of the dark, wooden pews but wondered if it would be seen as impolite. A sound from an alcove beyond one of the arches broke the silence.

"A hundred apologies," said the small man who emerged. He was clad in a long black gown, buttoned down the front, adorned with a large crucifix that swung in motion with his shuffling steps. Large, steel-framed glasses magnified his watery gray eyes. He shook their hands warmly, clasping each between his own, his smile wide beneath the expanse of beard that seemed to take up half of his torso.

He turned to Rebekah and reeled off a stream of explanations. From the corner of his eye, Ray caught a glimpse of Allegra, clad today in a sea-green tunic. Her eyes were wide, engrossed in the scene taking place, as though witnessing a myth come to life before her eyes.

Rebekah turned to them. "He says he's sorry for his English. He learned it in school and hasn't used it in half a century."

"We're sorry we can't speak anything else," replied Ray, his apology genuine.

"He's happy for us to record the Syriac liturgies?" Allegra asked.

"He is. He is delighted that there may be a way to rescue their ancient texts. They were very distressed when they found the words had vanished from their books of prayer. They have dedicated several hours in the day to pray for their return, and to seek forgiveness for any transgression that may have caused it," Rebekah translated. Father Yuhanna's face was grave, his eyebrows almost meeting his mustache.

They spent the day crammed in Father Yuhanna's small office at the back of the church. Much like Khadija's recitations of prophetic narrations the day before, Father Yuhanna's recital by heart of the church's book of prayer, *The Divine Liturgy According to the Rite of the Syriac Orthodox Church*, was also melodious. The warbling rhythms of the litanies and passages lulled Ray into a hypnotic trance, and at times he was unsure whether or not he was dreaming.

Allegra was far livelier, checking the readings on the equipment, saving the files whenever the priest reached a pause, at which point he would shuffle in his seat and push his glasses up over the bridge of his nose along which they had progressively slid. Rebekah had crept out to bring them flatbread wraps stuffed with crushed chickpeas and pickles, and cool bottles of still lemonade that they consumed ravenously.

~

"Another successful day of recording," said Allegra brightly as they climbed back into the carriage, the roofs opening over them once again as night fell. "Never in my life have I heard Syriac being spoken, and never would I have dreamed I'd spend an entire day hearing it." She sat back in her seat. Her eyes were clear, her expression enchanted, as though reliving the day before it had even ended.

"This is your specialty, no?" Rebekah leaned back from the front seat to ask her.

"It is," Allegra nodded. "Sacred manuscripts and historiography. I've spent my life reading and studying as many as possible. I suppose you could say I'm in my element here."

"And you, what is your specialty?" Rebekah turned to Ray. "Ray specializes in digital archiving," Allegra replied. "We really have him to thank for preserving them all."

Ray shook his head, grateful for once for the darkness and shadows that filled the streets. "Not really. I'm just..."

"He really is very good at what he does," Allegra insisted. Ray looked at her. She smiled and nodded. "It's true. And you, Rebekah, I'm simply in awe of your language skills. How many do you speak?"

Rebekah laughed. "Lots of people here can speak multiple languages, mainly Arabic and Hebrew. They are quite similar, actually, underneath. My advantage is my English, plus I also speak French and Spanish, though there's not much use for either nowadays."

"Sadly," Allegra sighed.

They met Fielding at the entrance to the Citadel. Though Ray was curious, he dared not ask what Fielding had spent his time doing, and something in him was not sure he would like the answer. His suit was rumpled and his jaw dark with stubble.

"I leave at nightfall tomorrow," Fielding told them, forgoing Elaina's offer of an evening meal. "I need samples from all three sets by then. You'll have them?"

"We will," replied Ray, unsure to whom Fielding had addressed the question exactly.

The final batch of samples they were due to gather from a set of Hebrew texts. The Jewish quarter was located in the southeast of the city. The oldest synagogue in Damascus, Rebekah told them, had been in Jobar, a town to the east of the city.

"Is that where we're going?" Ray asked.

"No, no. It was destroyed in 2014. Armed groups stormed the city. They looted it."

The first look of sadness that Ray had seen passed over her face.

"It was ancient, some say more than two thousand years old. And it was destroyed in a day." She swept back the wiry curls away from her forehead with a palm. "I often wonder what took its place, or whether they left it empty. I often hope they did. Its emptiness would tell a story. Don't you think?"

Neither Ray nor Allegra replied.

"Which synagogue are we going to?" asked Allegra, finally breaking the solemn silence that had filled the carriage.

"Oh!" Rebekah's face brightened. "We are not going to a synagogue. I forgot to tell you. We have been invited instead to the rabbi's home."

The idea of sitting for hours in a stranger's house would once have been unthinkable to Ray. Now, he felt only the memory of a sense of discomfort, which played around the edges of his mind.

The carriage would not fit down the narrow lanes, so the driver dropped them off as close as he could manage. They strolled through the tight alleys, the upper levels of the houses stretching out over the roads, their sandy-cement exteriors crumbling slightly as most things are apt to do with age. Children ran from the low wooden doorways, chasing balls and kittens who bounded down the dusty paths, and hid behind carts and crates, rolling around in the ecstasy and indignancy of being caught. Parents meandered in and out, half an eye on their spirited offspring, the rest on their chores.

They reached a small house next to an overflowing vegetable vendor, who called out the names and prices of his wares in sing-song tones. Beside him sat a toddler, whose cheeks were covered in sticky juices from the half-eaten fruit she held gleefully in her small fists.

A woman met them at the door. She was dressed in a skirt the color of eggplants and a white blouse, and had a faded floral scarf tied around her head. Esther, as she was introduced, greeted them pleasantly, asking their names in broken English. She seemed overjoyed by the presence of Rebekah, whom she greeted warmly, kissing both her cheeks.

"I've known her since I was a little girl," Rebekah whispered to them, somewhat bashfully.

She led them into a room upon which a cloth was laid in the middle of the floor, around which thick flat cushions were placed. Strewn across the cloth were various plates and platters, piled with fruits, breads, and preserves of numerous varieties. Esther gestured to the guests to sit.

They ate politely, tasting the breads dipped in the preserves, washed down with small glasses of tea. Ray was appreciative of the generosity, particularly in the light of the hardship Rebekah had described, though he could not stave off the thought that the more tea he drank the more he seemed to crave the familiar reassurance of a strong black cup of coffee.

Two children, a girl and a boy, the boy wearing a small cap at his crown, and the girl with her hair also wrapped like her mother's, came in to help clear away the dishes.

Having refilled their teacups, Esther sat back down opposite them on the low cushions.

"Shall we begin?" she asked.

Ray spent the rest of the day swallowing the intense sense of discomfort with his assumption that the rabbi they had been waiting for was Esther's husband. Esther, Rebekah explained, somewhat overdue, was the leader of a community of reformed Hasidic Jews who had fled from various places in Israel and the United States during the global conflict.

"I had no idea women could be rabbis in Hasidic communities, or that reformed Hasidic Jews even existed."

Rebekah laughed. "Very often people mistake tradition and the traditional. We certainly value tradition, but you'd be surprised at how untraditional many of our communities are. It was one of the things that earned us so many enemies."

Esther had dedicated herself to learning the scriptures when she was in high school and had been appointed as one of the first female rabbis in her community. She seemed to sway as she recited. Her consonants were sharper than the Arabic and Syriac, throaty. From time to time, her children joined her, harmonizing in the recitation of the parts they had learned.

"Her husband was killed in the war," Rebekah told them as they walked tiredly back down the narrow lanes. "He was tortured. They returned his body to her. But she never knew who did it. In the end it didn't matter. They were all as bad as each other."

~

"Mind if I join you?"

Allegra's shadowy figure, ethereal in an oat-colored gown, emerged from the stairwell up to the rooftop where Ray was sitting. The faintest flames of orange were just perceptible at the edges of the horizon. He had found a stone bench amongst some lemon trees. His vape was dangling from his fingertips, his wrists resting on his knees. The air was potent with jasmine and citrus.

He sat up, offering the vape to Allegra, who sat down next to him. She shook her head.

"I can't bring myself to use mine—it just tastes so artificial now."

Ray set it down on the arm of the bench. He, too, had noticed that the supposedly lemon-scented vapors smelled only metallic in among the fruits that hung around them, catching the lantern light on their shiny, dimpled skins.

"Did Fielding get off okay?" Ray had avoided him earlier that evening, having heard him come storming into the Citadel a little after they had finished their meal. The stomach-shrinking sense of embarrassment he felt in response to the man's presence in this place still returned at the memory of his loud, obnoxious demands, his refusal to don less conspicuous garb, his naked distaste for the food he was offered. His presence had the same spoiling effect as noticing a blot on a white shirt, a hair in a dish, or the knowledge of a looming deadline.

"He did." Allegra sighed. Ray was not sure whether it was one of relief or exhaustion, or both. "I gave him all the samples we collected."

"He'll be back in Freedom Point by tomorrow?" Fielding was the last thing Ray wanted to talk about, and yet, in his inability to express what it was that was on his mind, it was the only thing he could think of. And he feared that if he were to let the silence linger too long he may never be able to speak.

"Yes, before sunrise our time, I believe."

Allegra was also looking out over the intricate patchwork of the city, and the rough fields of the farmland beyond. The silence Ray feared hovered around them. A cool breeze brushed past, rippling the hems of their robes, and bringing with it voices from other rooftops nearby. In the large pool in the center of the roof garden, a pigeon was bathing, bobbing its head in and out from under its wings, scattering droplets that splashed with a flurry of notes back into the water.

"You know, when I was a little boy, I would read books under an oak tree on a hill behind our house." Allegra turned to look at him. He kept his gaze on the horizon. "Just silly sci-fi novels—you know how young boys do… Or did.

"I loved reading. I never realized that until today. It's something, I think, about the melody of the words." He paused, glancing toward her. The distant babble of voices ebbed and swelled as though echoing from the stones.

"I haven't loved anything in a very long time." It was not what he expected to say. He had never recalled even having had this thought prior to that moment. But he said it, spoke the words into the night air of Messiah City, and realized it was true. He realized it, sitting under a cluster of lemon trees, in a place he hadn't known existed, so far from his own home that he would never know how to get back.

In the dying light of the gloaming, he felt Allegra reach for his hand.

III

By the fourth day, Ray had begun to acclimatize to the dawn risings. The sounds of a city awakening poured in through the shutters along with the stirrings of sunlight.

He was hungry. His footsteps echoed through the stone corridors as though greeting him as he made his way to the dining room with the long wooden table. Allegra was already seated. He noticed that the dark black roots of her hair had begun to show, contrasting subtly against the shiny claret color of the rest that reached down to her shoulders.

The table seemed even more crammed than usual with offerings of olives, walnuts, fragrant and bitter pomegranate juices, and lemon preserves. Large, flat circles of speckled bread sat steaming under a linen cloth. Small platters of spreads topped with leafy herbs and drizzles of thick, shiny olive oil were arranged next to bowls of salty white cheese peppered with black nigella seeds. Rebekah, who had joined them yesterday, had explained that even before the ban on dairy production they had never farmed cattle; these climates were suitable only for sheep and goats. Their cheese was brined to preserve it. The salt, she had laughed, also stopped you from eating too much.

Ray sat down opposite Allegra, who handed him a small glass of tea. He felt a faint lurch in his chest as she smiled at him, but neither of them spoke. Mornings, he had realized long ago, were best spent in silence. It had never occurred to him that silence could be improved with company.

He scanned the table, unsure where to start. Allegra, he noticed, had wrapped her flatbread around a piece of white cheese, smeared with a spoonful of apricot jam. He reached for the cheese and jam and copied her. The bread, warm, melded the cool, salty cheese with the sticky preserve. His teeth sank through them blissfully, the union of sweet and savory exploding in his mouth. He washed it down with a gulp of the dark, tart tea.

Elaina appeared in the doorway, in the silent way Ray was becoming accustomed to. She was holding a large ceramic bowl, which was overflowing with large pieces of deep pink fruit. She smiled as she placed it on the table between them.

"Our first harvest of watermelon. Once these streets were full of watermelon sellers—they would pile them high in pyramids on the sides of the road." She spooned a large helping into two bowls and placed them before her guests. "You must try it with the cheese."

The pieces, firm at first and crunchy, dissolved in their mouths into a cool, sugary flood. Ray speared a piece of cheese on his fork and took another piece of the watermelon; the salt and the sweetness again deliciously confused him.

They were scheduled to visit the Grand Mosque of Damascus, the Umayyad Mosque as it was also known, to meet the orator who had learned countless books by heart. Ray bundled the heavy equipment bags into the back of the carriage with the help of Rebekah's uncle. The light was strong now that the sun had edged its way over the horizon and the scenes of the sky were incrementally disappearing beyond the creaking of the closing iron roofs.

As he reached for the final bag, Ray felt something vibrate. He unzipped it and rummaged around inside. It was his tablet. He had taken to packing it in among the recording things since it did not fit into the pockets of the linen suit he had been loaned. He slid it out from between two large boxes of cassette tapes and unlocked it.

A stream of notifications spewed across the screen. Ray blinked, realizing that the stones must have prevented them from arriving until they stepped out of the Citadel. He opened the first.

Urgent: Call immediately on secure line.

It was from Fielding. He ran through the rest of the messages.

Ray, call now. Secure line only. CALL NOW. URGENT!

RAY. WHERE THE FUCK ARE YOU? CALL IMMEDIATELY!

Ray looked up at Allegra, who had also been flicking frantically through her tablet. He hurried over to her.

"What's happened?" he asked her. She shook her head, still reading through the stream of alerts.

"I don't know." She frowned at the screen. "We should call."

Excusing themselves from Rebekah and her uncle, they walked around the courtyard at the front of the Citadel, holding their tablets aloft, trying to find the area with the strongest network connection. Ray pressed call.

"What the fuck are you two playing at?"

Fielding's face was enlarged, distorted by the angle of his tablet, but his anger was palpable through the screen.

"I beg your pardon," replied Allegra, calmly.

Ray's heart was pounding in his ears. "What's wrong?" he asked, trying to sound as relaxed as Allegra did.

"What's wrong? What's wrong?! You gave me dud tapes! Fucking empty tapes!" Fielding shook a cassette violently in front of the camera, streams of its acetate innards disgorged from the reel.

"Empty tapes?" Ray repeated. "That's impossible. We checked them all. And we made duplicate digital copies. Have you tried…?"

"I've tried fucking everything! You think I don't know how to play a recording? They're fucking blank! You wait… If I find out you're collaborating with those religious nuts…!"

Allegra took the tablet back from Ray. "Mr. Fielding," she said, sharply, coolly interrupting him. "We were extremely diligent in our recording operation. I'd appreciate it if you retracted your accusations and refrained from casting such aspersions."

"We will go back and check our copies," added Ray. "We'll let you know what we find and figure out a way to send you duplicates."

Fielding's face was thunderous. He was muttering dark threats under his breath. Ray added a few final words of reassurance as Allegra heaved the bags out of the carriage. She pulled out the recording tablets, setting them in a row on top of a low wall.

Ray ended the call—silence returned to the courtyard. Rebekah and her uncle stood watching them anxiously by the carriage, its door still open.

Allegra beckoned Ray toward her and handed him a set of earbuds, which he slotted into his ears. Allegra, her finger hovering over the button, looked at him. He nodded. Slowly, she pressed play.

Only twice in his life had Ray felt that heart-plummeting sense of fear—the sensation of a cavern opening up inside him and the entirety of his being collapsing into it.

The first happened in the moment he received the phone call from the hospital. It happened before he had even answered. He knew, instinctively, what he would hear the second the phone rang.

"Your father…"

The words themselves became a blur, an indistinct hum from the nurse on the other end of the line. He hadn't spoken; the world had simply caved in on itself.

In the courtyard, with Fielding's threats still ringing in his ears, Allegra had pressed play. The blank tapes and audio files had pitched their piercing silence into the empty air around them. With the terrifying sensation of that silence still under their skin, Ray and Allegra had spent the next hours frantically traveling from mosque to church to synagogue attempting to collect new samples from texts that were vanishing like sand through the narrow neck of an hourglass, tumbling into an eternity of absence.

As they had driven back to the Hadith School, Ray's head clamored with questions.

What? When? How? Who?

He had turned to Allegra, knowing that she would only agree with his questions, but seeking the sound of someone else's voice all the same. But she had slipped once again into the well of her own reflections.

Aminah looked concerned when they appeared, startled by Ray's hammering on the door. They had been more than willing to accommodate their request to repeat the previous day's session. Khadija, who had just arrived, was whisked again into the back room, hooked up to the equipment, and asked to begin. In silence, they had waited.

Ray's palms were hot. He scratched at them anxiously and ran a finger around his collar.

Khadija opened her mouth. She frowned, closed it, and shook her head.

The room was silent but for the faint churning of the cassettes recording nothing but their own hissing. She ran her hand over her face, rubbing her brow hard. She opened her mouth to try again, tears threatening at the corners of her eyes. But she could produce nothing but silence.

They had met the same look of horror in the priest's eyes when they arrived, the carriage screeching to a halt on the tarmac outside the church.

He flew out of the doors to meet them. He had stood to recite his prayers that morning. Every trace of the memory of his beloved texts had gone. By the time they left him, his beard was wet with tears.

The rabbi's daughter had answered the door. Her mother was deep in silent reflection, she said; she could not be disturbed. They tried the orator of the Grand Mosque, whom they had been scheduled to meet. He, too, could not remember a thing of the texts that he would often fall asleep reciting.

But the feeling Ray felt on that day was nothing compared to what he would feel the day after, when he and Allegra had sat in the early afternoon before Rabbi Solomon, to whom Esther's daughter had sent them. They had asked him to recite not from the secondary books, for both he and they knew by now that such a request would be futile. The entire city was tense with the attempt to remember. Rumors of the disappearance of words committed to heart had pulsated through the streets.

They asked the rabbi instead to read from the Torah, the Tanakh, the words he believed had been revealed to Moses, words that had been carved into stone.

"What would you like me to read?" he had asked.

"Anything," Ray had replied, afraid already of what was to come.

The rabbi cleared his throat and closed his eyes.

It had been the same with everyone they had asked. One never assumes one has forgotten. One assumes that something committed to memory can be summoned in an instant, that the mind is a safe box to which the owner alone holds the key. They would close their eyes, clear their throats, like they had every time they had opened that box in the past. But the key would not turn. They would frown, jiggle the lock. They would try again.

"Perhaps if you could tell me where to start?" asked the rabbi, trying to hide the growing fear that stretched his pupils wide.

"What about Exodus?"

He closed his eyes again. "Exodus," he repeated.

Ray braced himself. But that was not the second moment. The second instance of Ray's cavernous fear. It happened not when the rabbi could not remember. By that point, Ray's pulse had been racing, his mind riveted on convincing himself this was not all a dream.

The second moment happened, rather, when the rabbi reached to his shelf and took down his copy of the sacred text. It was then the world caved in.

~

Fear is an ancient thing, predating the oldest of words, the earliest of thoughts. It has been humankind's eternal ambition to eradicate it. In the absence of the elimination of fear, humans have sought to harness it.

The conflict that raged from 2033 to 2040 was a war of fear. It targeted everything that humans sought solace in—their homes, their freedoms, their own bodies, stripping them of their sense of certainty. In their attempt to restore calm and confidence, stability and sanity, Freedom Parliament sought to strike at the heart of fear; at uncertainty. Every action was recorded, every future action predicted. Nothing was left unknown. Diseases, cognitive conditions, the rate of mental and physical decline, the time and cause of death; everything was scheduled, awaited, anticipated.

What those in the towers of Freedom Point had not realized was that fear did not feed on uncertainty alone. There was another fear, a deeper dread, that the entirety of the free world was slowly being inflicted with. The fear of irrelevance, of a life devoid of mystery. The unknown is not only a source of fear, but a source of searching, a purpose. Meaning. As long as there was something to look for, there was something to live for. In eliminating the fear of uncertainty, the greatest fear of all was unleashed—the fear of meaninglessness.

In the moment that the rabbi opened the pages of his sacred text, sanctioned for ceremonial use by Freedom Point authorities, Ray was both certain and terrifyingly in the dark. His head was both quiet and clamoring with questions.

They rode quickly through the streets. People poured out of every door in a flood of panic that saturated the road. The air was thick with worry, tension. Ray felt his throat tighten.

"My uncle knows a shortcut back to the Citadel," Rebekah was shouting over the din and clamor that pounded off the sides of the carriage.

"The Citadel?" Ray asked. "Why are we going to the Citadel. We need to check other…"

"There's no need to check any other texts." Allegra spoke loudly. "Look…" Even as he had started his sentence, Ray had known she was right. A mass of people had swarmed around the church they were now passing. "It's happening to everyone."

"But why the Citadel?" Ray shouted over the loud commotion coming from the crowd.

"Elaina," replied Rebekah. "She will know what to do."

They clasped the edges of the carriage as Rebekah's uncle swerved down a small street and onto the large, empty road that encircled the city. The solid stone walls loomed up over them, capped in the iron roofs. On the furthest reaches of the city now, the noise had quelled. Much as blood rushes to vital organs in emergencies, the populace had pulsed inwards.

"Elaina?" repeated Ray. The ringing of the crowd in his head and ears was beginning to subside. The rhythmic clatter of hooves and the whooshing of the walls past the carriage soothing him out of the strain.

"Yes." Rebekah, whose face had been knitted with tension, let out a long sigh, her shoulders dropping. She turned to them. "She is the highest authority in the city. Ever since her arrival, people of all faiths have turned to her for… I don't know the word…"

"Guidance?" offered Allegra.

"Not quite. How do you say it…? Insight." She smiled, striking upon the word she was looking for. "In the early days, there was tension between some communities. Of course, no one would admit to it openly, but there was some discomfort amongst some people. Very few."

Allegra nodded. Ray was glad Fielding had not heard this. He knew that he would never have listened to a single word beyond this statement, adding it to his artillery of prejudices.

"But it was Elaina who resolved this. There was a famous story of a man who once confronted her, complaining that she had opened the Grand Mosque as a place of worship for all communities, so that they might pray side-by-side. He could share his city with other faiths, he said, but he should not have to share his mosque. He argued with her. No other faiths should be allowed in, he said.

"'The only person who should not enter any place of worship is a person who thinks others can be excluded from one.' That was her reply. The city has lived by it ever since."

The courtyard of the Citadel was teeming when the carriage finally arrived. The sun was setting, and the groaning of the roofs as they withdrew from each other added to the din of the growing commotion edging toward the Citadel doors. Believers of all denominations huddled in groups. A steady stream of people continued to pour into the walled space, many carrying books and scrolls, waving their empty pages aloft. The light that poured in submerged the congregating citizens in a deep orange glow. Groups of pigeons that had settled on the battlements of the Citadel took flight and alighted again in large swirls around its rooftops, as though carrying the worries below skywards.

Ray and Allegra jostled their way through the throngs of people toward the huge wooden doors. A harried-looking guard, who had been stationed there and who was earnestly trying to reassure swathes of distressed petitioners, spotted them. He hammered hard, three times, on the thick wood and the door swung open.

The noise outside faded as the door closed, and the iron lock fell into place behind them. Inside, the chamber that had not long ago taken Ray's breath away with its swooping stone arches and high domed ceiling was now the scene of a smaller gathering of hushed individuals. The wide echoing space, cool and airy, now seemed crowded with whispers and cluttered with heavy thoughts. They recognized Aminah, Father Yuhanna, Rabbi Esther, and the orator of the Grand Mosque along with what must have been the leaders of the many other groups they had, only a day before, been scheduled to meet.

The group turned as Ray and Allegra stepped in.

"You are here to see Elaina?" came the low questions. Ray and Allegra nodded.

"She is in prayer," another voice informed them.

Ray sat down next to Allegra on one of the low stone benches that encircled the room.

It was carved with grapevines and fig leaves. In the far corner, the nervous group remained. Some silent, deep in meditation, others discussing in whispered tones what they thought, hoped, Elaina might tell them.

Ray turned to Allegra, who, to his surprise, had pulled a book out of one of the bags she had been carrying. She was flipping quickly through the pages.

"Where did you…?"

"More questions," she smiled, not taking her eyes off the page. "I think, though…" She flipped faster, eventually finding the page she was after. "We may finally have an answer…"

She held the book open before Ray. There, in the middle of the otherwise empty page, to his surprise, he saw a verse. He turned to Allegra, confused. She flipped a few more pages and held up the book again. There was another.

"I thought they all disappeared," he said, watching her fingers flick through the pages swiftly.

"So did I," she replied. "So did everyone it seems." She looked up at the crowd still gathered at the opposite end of the hall. Just then, a shadow silently filled the doorway.

"If you'd like to follow me, my friends," came Elaina's calm, rippling voice.

They followed her into a chamber that led off the main hall, through a small arch that Ray had not noticed. Inside, the room was richly carpeted with rugs of intricate brocade. The ceilings were lower, carved ornately with beams of dark wood. A large bowl-shaped lantern hung in the middle of the room, the soft light streaming through its colored glass. They slid off their shoes at the entrance and Ray felt the firm woolen fibers against his feet.

Elaina took a seat on the floor, her legs folded under her, her hands on her knees. Ray and Allegra sat opposite, surrounded by the religious figures, their tension and anticipation palpable.

Elaina looked at them, scanning each face in turn silently. It seemed a long time before she spoke.

"A few days ago, I was contacted by the President of Freedom Point. She informed me that a number of digital copies of sacred texts had been corrupted. Of course, she wanted to know if I was aware of who might have done this. I reassured her that the last thing the people of Messiah City would want is for their texts to disappear; they live content in their way of life, even if it is only within these walls.

"I asked her to consider that she should ask not 'who' but 'how' these texts were disappearing. She took my response to mean an investigation into how it was that their state-of-the-art digital software security systems had been breached. But that was not my question. In asking how, I was asking her to examine the mechanics of this phenomenon. How was it unfolding?" She ran her hands over her thighs, smoothing her white tunic.

"I watched from a distance the texts disappearing one by one. First, verses, then entire books, then our voices, then our memories. There is a story in the *how*.

"And then, as the panic rose around the city, from the empty spaces that yawned across our pages and our minds, two verses presented themselves to me anew."

Elaina closed her eyes, and in a voice, crisp and melodious, she recited in Arabic two verses from the Quran. A gasp arose from the room at sounds that had been so utterly forgotten not moments before.

"'And We made the night and day two symbols,'" Elaina translated. "'And We erased the symbol of the night, and made the symbol of the day bright, visible for all to see.'"

A shiver ran down the back of Ray's neck, his hairs standing on end.

"'And when We withdrew Our verses and caused them to be forgotten, We rewrote them with words both similar and new.'" She opened her eyes and looked steadily around the room. "It is not our task to remember what has been taken," she said. "Look instead to what has remained."

The room was silent. Ray felt Allegra take his hand. "It's not an erasure, Ray," she whispered. "It's a rewriting."

The spoons tinkled on the small glass saucers as Ray carried the tray slowly, carefully, down the tiled corridor to the courtyard. The space was bathed in the delicate light of early evening, the roof overhead having parted to reveal the spattering of emergent stars.

He stopped at the entrance. Allegra was sitting at the small table, her head lowered over the outstretched pages of an open book, lit by the lantern hanging from its perch overhead. Her hair, now white, brushed the top of her shoulders and caught the light, which gave its silvery sheen.

It had not been a difficult decision for them to stay. They had made it in the same moment; separately, together. Fielding had been incensed by their attempt to explain. The idea that it had not been terrorism—that there was no enemy waiting to ambush them at the borders, that there was no chemical agent released into the archives, or radio waves causing selective amnesia—he took as both a personal and professional affront. Allegra, with a smoothness that never left her tone, had laid out the logic clearly.

"If that's what you believe," he had screamed, "then don't bother coming back."

With the electronic click of the call ending, Ray had known. The contrast between the options had never been clearer. What Ray had been missing in the free world, he had found here, in the dusty lanterned streets, ringing with calls to prayer and the voices of children, where rooftops sang with laughter and smelled of jasmine blooms. Where people waited.

What humanity did not know, seldom realized, was that the antidote to fear was not certainty, but desire. The only thing that could possibly overcome the feeling of being afraid was the feeling of wanting. And Ray had never wanted anything as much as he wanted to stay.

Ray set the tray down gently on the table. Allegra looked up at him and smiled, deep lines blossoming from the corners of her eyes. Ray sat next to her and placed his hand, the knuckles now gnarled and stiff, over hers.

As dawn had broken the morning after the final rewriting, the crowds had surged toward the Grand Mosque, coursing through the streets in a deluge of anticipation; their hands and eyes raised in repentance, in petition for answers. They filled the marble-floored courtyard and overflowed from every entrance. The pigeons circled high above.

"In the beginning was the Word," came the voice, echoing off the ancient stone that had seen civilizations rise and fall as far back as humans had recorded.

A hush fell over the crowd. They searched the skies to find the source of the voice, and saw Elaina standing on the terrace of the White Minaret, known as the Minaret of Christ. She was dressed in white, illuminated by the lights that shone from the minaret's peak. Ray and Allegra, who had followed the crowds from the Citadel, craned their necks to watch her.

"In the beginning was the Word, and the Word was from Us. And the Word assumed form." She paused; the pigeons fluttered. The silence that had descended reached into every corner of the city.

"To live a life blessed with anticipation; this is why we fled our homes and gathered here. We escaped violence and death. And most of all, we escaped the ever-expanding void of meaninglessness. And once here, we waited. In faith and grace, we waited."

She cast her arms out wide, as though encompassing the city at her feet in an embrace. "We were expecting the Messiah, a human, a man—here, on this very tower, we were promised his arrival. But as we waited, we were unexpectedly struck with fear. The sacred words that we had clung so closely to, the words we recited in our homes and repeated in our prayers, were suddenly withdrawn, erased, even from our very hearts."

A hushed ripple ran through the crowd.

"The erasure carried with it fear, an overwhelming fear. Fear always arrives with a question. Today, I will share with you the answer: No. We have not been forsaken; we have not been abandoned to the void. Through what has been erased, we have been spoken to again. The verses that remain are not remnants of an older message; they are the words of a new one. Through the absence, the presence of the Word has been revealed. The Word, as it was in the time before time, as it was before it became flesh. This is our message, one of a design all-encompassing, of a universe alive and one with the divine, of an end to the idols of stone and language, of a compassion that obliterates hatred, of a peace, of a promise. In the beginning was the Word. And in the end was the Word. The prophecy has been fulfilled. Our Messiah has indeed arrived."

~

The Messiah, the Word, would reign for a millennium, traditions had long told. This was how the city came to understand the fact that from the three sacred texts of the Abrahamic faiths—a total of over five hundred thousand words in their original scripts—only a thousand remained. Not in the languages in which they had been read, but in the language that everyone spoke.

Deeper still in those same traditions had lain a narration, memorized but misunderstood. It told of a night when scripture would be lifted, peeled away from the pages and hearts of people, until none of the verses were left.

In 2049, none of the old was left. As Elaina had explained, the entirety of what had been was erased. For a moment, everything had vanished from hearts, from minds, from pages, from screens, from history. In the next moment, with the return of only a thousand words, a new message was born, in the language humanity had chosen for itself: English. It was a message as old and as new as the universe. Those thousand words, now separated from the structures, even the languages that had supported them, could never be read in the same way again. It was as though three hues had been extracted and mixed on a canvas on which all other colors had been forgotten.

A calm had settled over the city, a serenity as the fearful storm passed and the clouds parted. A tranquility that spread, slowly, over the walls of the city, beckoning those who lay beyond them. Whereas once humanity had fled religion, they returned slowly to faith. They made pilgrimages to meaning, curious at first, hopeful. They saw, and they stayed. Messiah City swelled and spilled into the fields and flattened lands around it. Earnestly, its inhabitants built by moonlight and lantern.

What they sought now was not an arrival but an understanding, a study of the message, and an embodiment of the words. Though they committed them once again to heart, and filled their streets and homes with their recitation, they sought not to follow, to obey, for none of those words were left. Rather, they sought to see.

Ray lifted the cup from the tray and set it down before Allegra. They had been up since dawn, having climbed slowly in the light of swinging lanterns into the carriage still driven by Rebeka's uncle, who moved at the slower pace that time had gradually afforded them all, but who gave them the same smile he had greeted them with when they had climbed, uncertainly, into his carriage for the first time over thirty years ago.

Swaying along with the rhythm of the carriage, they had pressed dried fruit and handfuls of nuts into the palms of the children who trotted along gleefully beside them, as they too made their way toward the Grand Mosque.

Crowds were already gathering, just as they had done on this day in the year 2049, when Ray and Allegra had made the decision to stay, when all trace of thousands upon thousands of sacred words had disappeared, when the Messiah had arrived.

They picked their way slowly through the small groups of early comers, whose laughter and greetings rang around the courtyard and off the ancient stone. Every once in a while, a child would skitter in among the multitude of pigeons that milled about beside the Roman archway, sending a billowing curtain of birds up into the dawn air.

Over the years, a new tradition had grown, untraceable as most traditions were. To mark the dawn of the new message, the inhabitants of Messiah City would dress in black and white; white for the pages, black for the ink, the absence and the presence, the day and the night. Ray had chosen a black shirt and white trousers. At his chest, Allegra had pinned a sprig of jasmine. She had worn a black dress, embroidered at the cuffs, against which her silver hair shined. She straightened the flowers at Ray's chest as they neared the door.

In all corners of the square, vendors were setting up their stalls, lining up their produce for the waves of people who would soon congregate in every possible space in and around the Grand Mosque. The smell of roasting nuts, bubbling pots of corn, and freshly baked bread swirled through the air.

Rebekah, now with two children of her own, who peeped out shyly from behind her skirt, greeted Ray and Allegra at the door, stooping to pick up their shoes before they could bend, and placing them neatly in the racks. She kissed their cheeks and led them through the marble-floored courtyard, cool against their soles, and into the prayer hall.

The inhabitants of Messiah City had worked hard to repair the ancient details of the space, which had been ransacked during the years before the war. Together they had woven the rich red and gold carpets that lined the long expanse of the hall and repainted the beams in the high ceilings above in forest green. The chandeliers, which hung low, had been lit, casting the room in a deep golden glow.

Within the hour, the hall was full, the congregants spilling out into the courtyard and beyond. When Elaina ascended the pulpit, set into the marble interior walls, resplendent with their inlays of black, brown, and pink stone in geometric patterns that could spiral out for eternity, a hush once again descended upon the crowd, broken only by the cooing of pigeons and the murmurs of infants. She had changed little since they had first met, as she had emerged from the stone of the Citadel, as though already as old as the city itself. She was dressed in a gown of flowing black, a swathe of white fabric settled around her shoulders. She smiled at the sea of eager faces.

"In the beginning," she repeated, "was the Word." And with these words the recitation began.

In skin-quivering unison the words of the new message swelled up from the lungs of everyone present, rolling off the tongues of those who had committed it to memory and those who read from the copies that had been produced alike. The words resounded off the high marble pillars in a rumble whose vibrations permeated everyone present. The wave of words rose, higher and higher, deeper and deeper, until with its crescendo, silence settled once again like water over the gathered crowds.

In the quiet, a single note quivered. A young girl, upright, mouth open, eyes closed in concentration, was singing, standing on the final step of the pulpit. The note quavered in the air, strong, but fragile, as if at any moment it could be broken. Ray had felt the hairs on the back of his neck rise, as though the sound had run its fingers right over his skin. Suddenly, from the furthest end of the hall, next to the Shrine of John the Baptist, came another, a boy who sang the note with her. From another corner, another note, until from a dozen places around the room came the harmony of children singing.

The ceremony had ended, as it always did, with a moment of silent reflection, a time to recount the events of another year spent in the era of a new message, to remember those who had not seen the year through, to gather the pieces of oneself inevitably scattered throughout the months.

Ray reflected on all he could remember, now in the eighty-fifth year of his life, a year after predictions had once foretold his demise. He cast his mind over all he could recall of the thirty years he had spent in Messiah City, working in their archives, categorizing and storing safely all those texts that had been left—treatises on medicine, ancient histories, poetry, and fables—his rough skin whispering over the paper as he wondered about the lives of those who'd inked their words.

As they departed, a slow babbling stream of joyful crowds, each person had been handed a soft, pillowy pink rose, whose fragrance oozed from its center, such that soon the square hummed with the floral scent. Allegra had clipped hers into her jade clasp that pulled back one side of her hair from her face. Ray clipped his next to the jasmine. Outside, the crowds had been joyful. A festive spirit had buzzed around the square and into the sheltered market streets that channeled away those looking for gifts and treats to fill their tables.

They spent the day visiting familiar faces with whom they had built and shared a history: Esther, Aminah, the children of Father Yuhanna, many of whom now had families of their own, to whom they bought gifts, and whiled away several pleasant hours in comfortable chatter, eating from the large table of food, at the center of which sat the swirls of bread, in which black and white sesame seeds were intertwined.

It had been a fulfilling day, the type that filled Ray and Allegra both with a warm, contented weariness, the promise of sleep, still early, playing at the corners of their consciousness. They had walked back through the dusk, slowly introducing its shadows as the roofs yawned open. The stillness of their tranquil courtyard now was soothing.

Somewhere, a songbird was warbling.

Allegra sat back in her chair, and with her eyes closed, lifted the cup to her lips. Reaching for his own, Ray felt the gentle heat through his fingertips. He cradled the warm glass in his palm. Sounds from the rooftop gardens trickled into the courtyard, aglow with the soft light of the evening. The melodies of the voices mingled with the fountain that babbled at its center, the ripples in its crystal-clear surface catching the lantern light, casting sparkling shafts in every direction. In the raised tiled basin at its center, two birds were washing their wings. Ray stirred his spoon in the glass, adding to the symphony of the scene. He took a sip of the sweet, dark tea.

"I often wonder—" Allegra smiled, as she pulled the book before her slowly toward him, and smoothed out the pages with her hands. It was bound in leather, thick and green, the words inside inked in black, the words on the spine imprinted in gold. *The Book of We*. Ray inhaled the evening breeze and leaned over the pages. He could smell jasmine blossoms and the faintest scent of almond.

"I often wonder," Allegra repeated, "how much of us was rewritten too."

The Book of We

In the beginning,
    We became.
        The heavens, the earths, the universe.
And Earth was yet a formless thing.
    And over the depths of its surface, darkness.
        And in the dark,
            We moved.

We desired.
    "Let there be light."
    And from the darkness,
        of the darkness,
            came light.

And from the elements,
We extracted intelligence.
    And it evolved,
        Ever closer to Our image,
            Conscious
            Dexterous
            Articulate.

Evening passed, and morning came.
This was the sixth day.

And on the seventh,
    We paused.

            We observed everything We had become,
            and We were pleased.

Arise, O beautiful ones,
And see.

Winter is past;
The season of sight has come.

In Us you will see the shepherd,
And in Us you will see the flock;

In green pastures, We lay you down,
leading you beside quiet waters,
to restore your desperate minds.

To each of you is your path,
which you follow in Our Names, Our design.

Even as you walk
through the harshest of valleys,
with every step, it is Us you will find.

Blessed are the gentle,
For they have inherited the earth.
Blessed are those who hunger and thirst for purpose,
For it has been found.
Blessed are the merciful,
For they have received.
Blessed are the clear of sight,
For they will see.
Blessed are the peacemakers,
For they have prevailed.

And so, We tell you,
Keep on asking, and you will receive.
Keep on seeking, and you will find.
Keep on looking, and you will see.

For everyone who asks, receives.
Everyone who seeks, finds.
And everyone who looks will be shown.

Was there not a time
in the history of Time,

when humankind were not?

From elements paired,
 The human emerged
  Empowered with hearing and sight,

Thus, were they qualified for the journey of life.

By the land of the fig and the olive,
We drew forth the human in perfected measure
 Placing within them the freedom to self-destruct.

We presented the trust of perception
 To the mountains,
 the plains,
 and the skies,
  But before it, they quavered and declined.

But the human embraced this distinction,
 For until then,
  they had been unknowing and blind.

O consciousness contended,
 Tranquil in its certitude,
  Ever returning to Us,
   Beheld and beholding.

Become of Our own
 And abide within Our home.

Say,
 The human mind is designed
  to relate to a singular locus
   A self-sustaining, perpetual lens
   Neither inferred, nor implied.
      Unparalleled.

There is, in the design of the universe
 and the alternation of the day and night

Clues for thirsty minds

And We made the night and day two symbols,
    And We erased the symbol of the night
        And made the symbol of the day bright, visible
        for all to see.

And when We withdrew Our verses and caused them to
be forgotten,
    We rewrote them with words both similar and new.

In the beginning was the Word,
      and the Word was from Us,
           And the Word assumed form.

In the beginning was the Word,
      And in the end
           was the Word.

And now, a special excerpt from Omar Imady's next novel…

The Weight
of
Waiting

The knock I've been dreading all morning comes twelve minutes late.

"We had some trouble finding the place…"

The "place" is my apartment. Perhaps I should have clarified that on my website. The "we" includes Mrs. Morales—"Camilla," she elaborates with long, stretched syllables and a loose handshake—and her immediately eager daughter Flora, who is clenching armfuls of rustling satin skirt about her torso. Her dress is violet. It's not the "color I would have chosen for her. I imagine she chose it herself. You work from home…" Camilla appears to be confirming this to herself rather than asking me. She scans the small entrance hall, taking languid stock of the four rooms that constitute my "studio." "Should I go in here?" Flora has already bustled her way through the doorway to the living area, which I don't really live in but where my equipment is set up.

Camilla is twiddling a large rock of a diamond ring that hangs loosely between her knuckles. I desperately wish my hands hadn't been damp from having washed them after my third trip to the bathroom, my subconscious attempts, I'm sure, to rid myself in some way of the unavoidable anxiety and existential dread that precedes every miserable photoshoot.

"It's for my daughter's quinceañera," she'd written in her email. I'd had to look that up. A fifteenth birthday celebration, popular in South America. She didn't look fifteen. She looked much younger.

I run my hands nervously through my hair, the lurking specter of premature regret now surging through up my esophagus. I'd hated the idea even when I'd confirmed the appointment, on so many levels. Right now, primarily so because Flora is already sitting expectantly on the small couch opposite the tripod with a camera-ready smile. This is clearly not her first rodeo. I am reminded of how acutely uncomfortable I am with the idea of photographing people who want to be photographed.

I'm also extremely uncomfortable with the fact that Camilla has made her way languorously not into the studio but into the kitchen area, separated from the room by a low partition, and is examining the cups on the shelf. Her shoes make slow clicks on the gray faux floor tiles. Her hair is the color of freckles, and it falls in elegant, well-behaved waves around her shoulders. She looks like she walked straight off the page of *Town and Country*. She twirls a chipped mug in her fingertips, quite like one might examine a potential purchase in an overpriced gallery. She sets it back down slowly on the shelf and moves over to a bowl of cherries I'd forgotten about on the back corner of my kitchen counter. The absurdity of the scene strikes me suddenly. Not with the hilarity that Camus might suggest it is seen, but an uneasiness in the face of such a bizarre arrangement.

"Mummy." Flora's interruption is whining and already impatient. Her shoulders droop slightly from their anticipatory poise.

"Yes, darling…?" Camilla doesn't turn her head. I'm afraid she's about to open the fridge. I'm not sure my dignity could withstand another slow scan.

"Should we get started? Perhaps?" I'm hovering at the border where kitchen tiles meet carpet. Flora ruffles herself back into position on the couch. Camilla finally turns. "Maybe if you sit here?" I beckon to a chair in the corner of the living room studio, still hovering. I know the rules all too well. The unspoken rules of male photographers. It used to be "never be caught with your pants down." Now it's "don't even have your hands near your belt." It never ceases to surprise me the risks photographers will still take. What they are willing to suggest they have seen. I am convinced anyone now who photographs women, or men for that matter, in the nude has a death wish; the kamikazes of the art world. Photographs are, after all, evidence. Incrimination. And the burden of proof is always on the photographer to tell the story of what happened outside of the frame. I am the first to provide the benefit of the doubt, but I know that favor will not be returned.

"Mr. Hadleigh, on July 6th of the year in question you photographed one Flora Morales, then aged fifteen." A photograph appears on the screen to the right of the judge. "Miss Morales claims that after this photograph was taken, during a brief period in which her mother left the room, you proceeded to…" Or worse yet, there is no court case.

I can envision the headline, thirty years from today, accompanied by a picture of a girl in a cake-topper purple dress sitting on a sofa in my studio, captioned "Kiddy-fiddler photo man's first victim. He waited until my mother went for a pee."

"Mrs. Morales, if you could just take a seat." I'm almost pleading. The sooner she sits, the sooner I can step into the living room and get this over with.

I am surprised at Camilla's disinterest. Her apathy is toward the bouncing girl on the couch, who is clearly desperate to be fawned over and immortalized in her extravagant outfit. She seems far more interested now in the books on the small coffee table in front of her, although *interested* is possibly an exaggeration. She flicks through them slowly with a long finger, one leg folded neatly over the other, her other hand settled on her knee over the crisp crease of her navy trousers. A gold watch dangles out from the cuff of her shirt. Her wrists are striking—narrow and angular. I hate the word *delicate* but I struggle to think of a better description. What on earth was this woman doing in my "studio" commissioning quinceañera pictures about which she clearly couldn't care less?

"How do I look?"

I bend to lens level, looking at Flora through the safety of the camera. How do I tell her? How do I tell her I'd rather be photographing trees? Ants on a sticky pavement, people at a bus stop, a fluttering crisp packet jiving down the esplanade in the sickly heat. I focus my lens. She's fiddling with her thick, dark hair, held up in a complicated pile, garnished with flowery hair clips. "If you could just put your hands on your lap and turn your head towards me." I hear another slick glossy page flip from the corner of the room.

"Mummy."

"Yes, darling… You look beautiful."

Flora beams. *Click*. On some textbook level that one will be a good picture at least. Flora looks expectantly at the camera. One-click is clearly not enough.

"Maybe I should lie on the couch?"

I emerge quickly from behind the lens.

"Something like…" She reclines clumsily on the couch cushions, one leg dangling off the side. She props her head up with one arm.

"No, no." I wave my hands.

Definitely *no* lying on the couch pictures. That would be the first nail in the coffin. "Why don't you stand up?" Camilla does not look up from the page, Dorothea Lange's encapsulation of the Great Depression of 1936—a black and white picture of a thirty-two-year-old mother and her two starving children—one of the most famous photographs of the twentieth century. Camilla flicks the page again. I retreat back behind my lens. I make a point this time of clicking plenty. I direct Flora to the window, and fiddle with my lighting. I added a few extra clicks for good measure.

Sensing movement from the corner of the room, I look over to Camilla, who is now standing. Her crisp creases have fallen back into their immaculately vertical position. She steps slowly toward me.

"Oh no, no, no." My response startles her. For the first time, a semblance of expression passes over her face, her eyebrows lift slightly. "Um…" I fumble for a credible excuse. "It's broken."

"Your bathroom is broken?" Her eyebrows are still raised.

"Yes, out of order. I'm waiting for the plumber. He was supposed to come yesterday, but you know how they are."

"I just want to wash my hands…" I wonder if she might not want to inspect my bathroom cupboard.

"The taps are broken—it's all broken." I can see the lawsuit happening already. She must not leave the room.

"The taps are broken…" She cocks her head and repeats this back to me, perhaps only to accentuate quite how incredulous this is beginning to sound. I maneuver myself between her and the door. I don't care. She's not leaving me alone with a fifteen-year-old.

"We're almost finished here—we just need a few more minutes."

"Mummy, you said this wouldn't be boring. I told you we should have gone to London. Maria went to London for her quinceañera. We should have gone to London—you never listen," Flora drones, sounding like a fly buzzing.

Camilla, mercifully abandoning her attempts to leave the room, swoops up a stray curl that has escaped the strictures of Flora's hairspray and sighs, fixing it back into place. She tilts up her daughter's chin with the knuckle of her forefinger. Her watch jangles quietly on her wrist.

"Can't we do it on the beach? It's just over there. Daddy would love pictures of me on the beach."

At least there's one piece of the puzzle. This entire endeavor must be at the behest of Mr. Morales, or at least it is for his benefit.

Camilla cocks her head; her hair falls away from her face slightly. She's wearing small pearl earrings. Her finger is still propping up the girl's chin. "Daddy does love the beach…" She turns to me, her face now questioning. She pauses. "I'd pay extra, of course…"

It's tempting. "Extra" would cover my rent for another month, I'm sure, and though I want nothing more than for them to leave, to clamber back into whatever 4x4 they arrived in, and to head back to whatever nine-bedroom house they came from in Thorpe Bay, I don't want to disappoint her. Not Flora. I have no problem disappointing Flora. Flora needs to learn someday soon that life will be full of disappointments, no matter how much you or Daddy are willing to pay. But something in the way she holds her head at that moment, the bright noon sun catching her shoulders through the window, tells me that Camilla has already met her fair share of hers. Plus, at least we'd be in public. No threat of lawsuits there, as far as I know.

I wonder if "Daddy" knew that Southend's beach was more of a marine toilet bowl when he moved here. It lies at the yawning mouth of the Thames estuary, and its scummy waters lap only lazily at the crummy sandy shores, and that's when the tide is in. I realize, as we make our way down the stairs of the apartment building, the legs of my tripod clattering behind me, that I should have checked the tide times, and pray there is a beach at all. What only locals know is that the tides here are so extreme that often there is either no beach, and the waves slap almost against the pavement, or there is no water, having receded so far from the shore that only foamy rivulets and pathetic little pools are left in the graying sand. Thankfully, it is at least passable as a beach today, and though the sand is littered with people and their detritus, beseeching the sun to tan their blubbery bodies, there is a clear spot further down the esplanade where I can set up shop.

Flora trots down the beach, skirt in arms, curls escaping at will now from their coiffured cage. Camilla walks ahead of me. She has taken off her shoes and is carrying them by the lip of their heels. She picks her way through the bodies and fish and chip cartons, ice lolly sticks and discarded beer bottles. My camera bounces off my chest as I navigate my way behind her, ignoring the thudding R&B from teenagers' speakerphones.

Flora has flicked off her shoes too. They land in the sand like coconuts. She splashes into the beige water's edge. "Take a picture of me in the sea!"

A few sunbathers crane their necks up from their beach towels and deck chairs to watch the scene; the girl in a purple satin meringue, kicking up the water with her toes, her skirt now up around her thighs, and an immaculately dressed woman and a badly dressed photographer in toe. I set up my tripod, ignoring them as best I can, glad only for their presence as "the public." Camilla has identified a spot relatively clear of human leftovers and has sat down, her knees bent, her arms behind her, propping herself up in the shape of a fluid M. Her hair has fallen away from her shoulders, down her back.

"That's lovely, darling..." she calls to Flora, to whom she is still paying no attention. From my stooped position behind the camera, I can tell she is looking out toward the sea, where the land finally falls away and all is ocean.

"Maybe I can do a cartwheel?" Flora raises her hands in the air and rotates herself clumsily into the shallow water, her knees bent at awkward angles, and her feet flicking up splodges of sand. I click frantically. At least it's not sitting on a sofa; at least it's different. At least it's in public.

Both Camilla and I, *I realize,* are fully aware that this shoot will not be over until Flora has thoroughly enjoyed herself, milked every ounce of attention from anyone in the vicinity, so stopping her now spinning in circles in the dirty waves, or pretending to dive, is utterly futile and counterproductive. I am simply here to stand and snap. Her mother is here simply to be her mother, it seems, offering occasional tidbits of approval and facilitating her attempts to win Daddy's affections.

I'm bored of the close-up shots of Flora's now overly familiar face. A wider lens might provide some variety to the shots. I wonder what they would make of photographs that capture not only Flora's quinceañera glee but the ogling bemusement of her fellow singed beachgoers. That might at least make for an interesting picture.

I zoom out wide. Camilla emerges, blurrily at first, into the frame. She has not moved from her position, at all except, I notice, she is now looking at me. Or rather the camera. Straight down the lens. I pause, waiting for her to turn away, to realise that it was in actual fact something behind me that caught her attention. But there is no mistaking that look, you can tell when someone is looking at a camera, whether in a photograph or on television. It is unnerving, when a character looks straight down the lens, breaking the fourth wall, intruding into your gaze, into whatever lies behind it. I feel the hairs on the back of my neck rise. Flora is waving her arms in time to the Justin Beiber song that is now blasting out of the speaker phones, and a flock of seagulls are fighting over a half-eaten bag of chips in the distance. Camilla still has not looked away. Dare I?

I adjust the camera angle ever so slightly and zoom in slowly. *Click.*

I could have sworn she smiled.

IN THE YEAR 1966...
A MOTHER GIVES BIRTH,
A CONFIGURATION OF ANGELS ASSEMBLES,
AND A GOLDEN SCROLL IS OPENED.
A RIDDLE IS BORN.

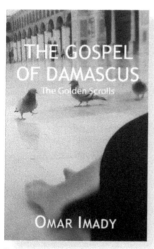

The story follows the life of Yune Bukhari, a young Syrian man, as he prepares for the Second Coming, secretly guided by eight angels – serious and strange, flamboyant and fascinating – who solve seven cryptic commands contained in golden scrolls which gradually reveal their mission on earth.

The Gospel of Damascus: The Golden Scrolls is a renowned work of literature translated into several languages. Omar Imady takes us on a journey that unites people of all faiths, providing a profound perspective on individual truths, spirituality, and humankind as a whole. The novel offers a message of optimism for all ages, one which is especially relevant to the challenges of our modern world.

A LYRICAL SYMPHONY OF
THREE CAPTIVATING MOVEMENTS:
THE PASSION OF SIDRA,
THE SEDUCTION OF JUDE,
&THE RAGE OF FATIMA.

Three stories come together with the light touch of magical realism to examine, interrogate, and challenge our understanding of universal truths and spirituality…

An English nurse becomes possessed with unraveling the mystery behind the disappearance of a Syrian woman in the twilight town of King's Lynn, stumbling along the way upon a history and present replete with magic and mysticism.

A Syrian professor escapes Damascus only to find himself in another surreal and dangerous setting, uncovering a conspiracy that places his life in even greater peril.

An Oxford scholar and an eccentric Syrian journalist embark on an adventure through Portugal and Spain, seeking to decipher an ancient manuscript and uncover a religious conspiracy with explosive personal and universal implications.

**WHEN MODERN SCIENCE FAILS
TO SAVE HIS WIFE CELESTE,
MICHAEL TURNS TO RELIGION.
WHEN RELIGION FAILS TO CURE HER,
HE IS LEFT SEARCHING FOR ANSWERS.**

From Michael's grief flows anger, determination, and finally the plan – a meticulous experiment to unravel the truth in one of civilization's most controversial topics … the concept of God.

At the heart of this plan is Hamida Begum. A young woman of depth and intelligence, heiress to a lost lineage. Selected and prepared. Qualified in ways even Michael could never have anticipated. Will her involvement in this vast, mysterious, and at times unethical endeavor deliver resolution?

The Celeste Experiment is the story of one man's attempt to sever the spiritual threads of history once and for all. It is a thrilling journey of revenge and conviction, sorrow and rage, design and entrapment, and the message of whispered words. A tale where no one and nothing is vindicated … except love.

WELCOME TO THE GAME, CAITLYN.
PASSWORD REQUIRED.
HINT:
IF YOU'RE NOT SMART ENOUGH
TO GUESS THE PASSWORD,
YOU'RE NOT SMART ENOUGH TO PLAY.

Gifted with an extraordinary mind, a ravenous appetite for knowledge, food, and women, Caitlyn thrives on challenges.

In her last hours as a student at Yale, she receives a mysterious invitation. One she cannot refuse. Selected by a panel of twelve of the world's greatest minds in her field, Caitlyn is invited to play a game - a unique contest of knowledge based on a series of expertly crafted questions.

The search for answers takes Caitlyn on a journey, both existentially and around the world. As she continues to follow the clues and her investigation into historical archives deepens, she is unexpectedly pulled further into the mystery of her own traumatic past.

The challenge of winning the game quickly escalates into a personal mission of uncovering who, or what, is asking the questions, and why.

Clarinet

ROBBIE WILLIAMS

SWING WHEN YOU'RE WINNING

Folio © 2001 International Music Publications Ltd

Production
Anna Joyce

Photography
Hamish Brown

Arrangements and CD production
Artemis Music Ltd

I WILL TALK AND HOLLYWOOD WILL LISTEN

Words and Music by Robert Williams and Guy Chambers

Track 2

Backing

MACK THE KNIFE

Words by Bertholt Brecht
Music by Kurt Weill
Translation by Marc Blitzstein

IT WAS A VERY GOOD YEAR

Words and Music by Ervin Drake

Backing

SOMETHIN' STUPID

Words and Music by Carson Parks

Track 5
Backing

DO NOTHIN' TILL YOU HEAR FROM ME

Words by Bob Russell
Music by Duke Ellington

Track 6
Backing

STRAIGHTEN UP AND FLY RIGHT

Words and Music by Nat King Cole and Irving Mills

Backing

14

THINGS

Words and Music by Bobby Darin

Track 8
Backing

WELL, DID YOU EVAH

Words and Music by Cole Porter

Medium swing

relaxed swing quavers

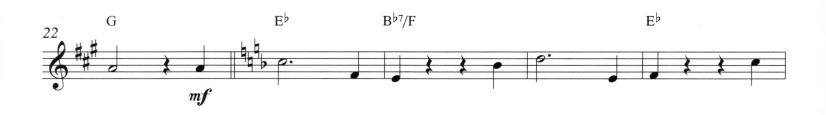

MR. BOJANGLES

Words and Music by Jerry Jeff Walker

Backing

ONE FOR MY BABY

Words by Johnny Mercer
Music by Harold Arlen

AIN'T THAT A KICK IN THE HEAD

Words by Sammy Cahn
Music by Jimmy Van Heusen

Backing

HAVE YOU MET MISS JONES?

Words by Lorenz Hart
Music by Richard Rodgers

Backing

ME AND MY SHADOW

(AS PERFORMED BY SAMMY DAVIS, JR. AND FRANK SINATRA)

Words by Billy Rose
Music by Al Johnson and Dave Dreyer

Backing

BEYOND THE SEA

Original Words and Music by
Charles Trenet and Albert Lasry
English Words by Jack Lawrence

Track 15
Backing

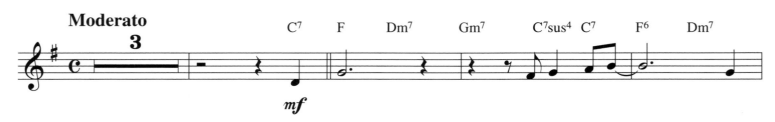

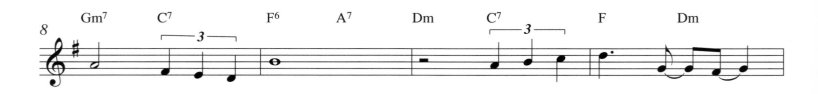

THEY CAN'T TAKE THAT AWAY FROM ME

Music and Lyrics by George Gershwin and Ira Gershwin

Piano/Vocal/Guitar
Order Reference: 9237A
ISBN: 1-84328-035-3

I WILL TALK AND HOLLYWOOD WILL LISTEN
MACK THE KNIFE
SOMETHIN' STUPID
DO NOTHIN' TILL YOU HEAR FROM ME
IT WAS A VERY GOOD YEAR
STRAIGHTEN UP AND FLY RIGHT
WELL, DID YOU EVAH
MR. BOJANGLES
ONE FOR MY BABY
THINGS
AIN'T THAT A KICK IN THE HEAD
THEY CAN'T TAKE THAT AWAY FROM ME
HAVE YOU MET MISS JONES?
ME AND MY SHADOW
(AS PERFORMED BY SAMMY DAVIS, JR. AND FRANK SINATRA)
BEYOND THE SEA

Available from all good music shops

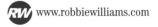 www.robbiewilliams.com

LIFE THRU A LENS

Piano/Vocal/Guitar
Order Reference: 5853A
ISBN: 1-85909-540-2

LAZY DAYS
LIFE THRU A LENS
EGO A GO GO
ANGELS
SOUTH OF THE BORDER
OLD BEFORE I DIE
ONE OF GOD'S BETTER PEOPLE
LET ME ENTERTAIN YOU
KILLING ME
CLEAN
BABY GIRL WINDOW

I'VE BEEN EXPECTING YOU

Piano/Vocal/Guitar
Order Reference: 6645A
ISBN: 1-85909-628-X

STRONG
NO REGRETS
MILLENNIUM
PHOENIX FROM THE FLAMES
WIN SOME LOSE SOME
GRACE
JESUS IN A CAMPER VAN
HEAVEN FROM HERE
KARMA KILLER
SHE'S THE ONE
MAN MACHINE
THESE DREAMS
STAND YOUR GROUND
STALKERS DAY OFF

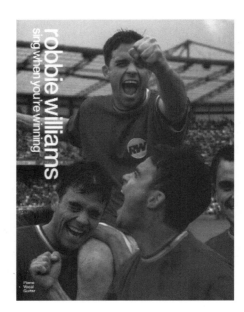

SING WHEN YOU'RE WINNING

Piano/Vocal/Guitar
Order Reference: 7591A
ISBN: 1-85909-927-0

LET LOVE BE YOUR ENERGY
BETTER MAN
ROCK DJ
SUPREME
KIDS
IF IT'S HURTING YOU
SINGING FOR THE LONELY
LOVE CALLING EARTH
KNUTSFORD CITY LIMITS
FOREVER TEXAS
BY ALL MEANS NECESSARY
THE ROAD TO MANDALAY

Available from all good music shops

 www.robbiewilliams.com